Author's Note

These Cascadia Wolves novel/novella reissues enable me to bring back a series I've loved since day one. Some of the earlier books had been unavailable for a few years, so I'm thrilled to be able to bring them back with some neatening, tightening and updated covers.

The stories have not changed from the original editions. The editing and revision I've done was to hopefully make the stories easier to read and stronger overall, but the core of the story remains the same.

Ray—
because you're the model for so many of my heroes!

BONDED PAIR

Chapter One

Dear God, kill me now. Megan Warden pretended to sleep rather than engage with her insane mother and listen to her prattle on and on about men, children and pregnancy as she had for the past seven hours. Seriously, the military should look into using Beth Warden for interrogation. No terrorist could ever hold up under this stuff.

"I was telling Grandma, there are going to be many single wolves at this event, Megan. Who knows who you might meet," her mother repeated for the thousandth time.

Megan kept her head down, her chin against her chest and tried to regulate her breathing. She'd been drinking "special" coffee all day long but werewolf physiology meant the alcohol wore off relatively soon.

So her mother continued talking, knowing Megan wasn't really asleep but Megan kept pretending anyway. Oh the little games you play with family.

"You can't hide under those dark glasses forever," Layla cracked from her place next to Megan. They hurtled down the road in the huge SUV her older brother Lex had arranged for them. She'd taken the farthest row back, hoping her mother and grandmother would get into the other car in this caravan of horrors but no, they both decided to ride in this one.

"Shut the fuck up. You're married and you've bred. You're the freaking golden child." She kept her head down and her voice low but they'd hear her anyway. Damned wolves.

"Megan, did you just say the *F* word?" Her grandmother tsked at her. She had a twinkle in her eye as she said it, proving she was just as much a Warden as the rest.

"She started it." Megan knew she sounded petulant but she was past doubting her sanity, and full throttle into cursing her life.

Tracy snorted out a laugh and not for the first time, Megan wondered why in the hell she'd agreed to take a road trip to a wedding with her mother, grandmother and her *married* sisters.

Because she was the Enforcer of the Cascadia werewolf pack and it was the only way Lex would agree to them going without a full escort of armed wolves. As it was, Dave, her cousin and her sister-in-law Grace's personal bodyguard, was there in the car behind them along with two other guards.

And okay, so she did love her family, and her sisters were all in from out of town and she didn't see them nearly often enough. On paper, *conceptually*, it sounded like fun to hang out with the Warden women for a week or so.

Stuck in a car with them for hours on end? Not so much with the fun.

"Can we stop sometime soon? I have to pee." Tracy ran a hand over her belly and smiled at Megan. "Maybe

she'll stop for a few minutes." She winked and Megan
rolled her eyes.

"We should be stopping for the day at some point
anyway. Tracy has got to be uncomfortable and
Grandma needs to rest." Beth turned around in the
seat. "Oh you're awake now!" she said when she caught
Megan with her eyes open.

Damn. The woman was diabolical.

"I think we should at least get to the California bor-
der before we stop. And I'm fine. I'm just pregnant for
goodness' sake. But dinner would be nice. I'm hungry."
Tracy's lips quivered, barely holding back laughter.

That suggestion met with enthusiasm and Tegan
called out that she'd pull over in the next town.

Their noisy group took over pretty much the entire
small-town Oregon restaurant. Megan wanted to laugh
at the picture they all made. Boisterous, happy, all of
them emanating that vibrant otherness Weres seemed to.

"Why are you bogarting the catsup?" Tegan demanded.

"Just to annoy you apparently." Megan shoved the
bottle at her sister with a smirk. She looked back over
to her mother, pasting sincere-looking concern on her
face. "You know, you might be more comfortable in the
other car with Dave. You can feel the road more in our
car I think. You and Grandma both."

Dave kicked her but it was every werewolf for herself.

Nina laughed from down at the other end of the table
but didn't offer her opinion on the matter. Better for
her anyway as Megan was her bodyguard as well as
the pack Enforcer. One suggestion from Megan to Lex

about Nina's safety and suddenly her sister-in-law would have to go everywhere with three bodyguards.

"Well, aren't you sweet? But we're fine. We'll be stopping for the night soon enough and I don't get enough chance to visit with Grace and Tegan now that they're on the other side of the country." Her mother smiled, patting Megan's hand.

She'd go in the other car herself but with Grace and Nina along, that was two Alphas, including *the* Supreme Alpha, so as the Enforcer, Megan needed to be there. Gah.

"Here, Beth, have I shown you the pictures of little miss I've-got-my-daddy-wrapped-around-my-finger? Last month we took her for her first haircut and I think Cade might have cried." Grace, her sister-in-law and current savior, grinned at her before turning her attention back to Beth. "I know he baked two dozen cookies when we got home."

The pictures began to circulate from several directions and Beth eased back, happily engrossed in her grandbabies. For the moment, Megan let herself relax and enjoy the people who vexed and charmed her most in the universe.

After another several hours, they finally pulled into a hotel off the freeway and Megan skipped the late-night pie and ice cream and headed to the room with Tracy and the bags. Nina would be right next door but no one in their right mind roomed with her but Lex. Nina was not a fun roommate, she was nosy, never shut up and thought fart jokes were hilarious.

"You did a good job with her today, you know. She just wants you to be happy but I remember how hard it was to be her target." Tracy groaned as she put her feet up on the bed in the hotel room she shared with Megan.

"I know she does, Trace. But hello, do you think it's my choice? This whole wolf-mate thing is sort of out of my hands. Plus, kinda busy you know? Being Enforcer is a big job. I don't have the time Mom does to think up ways to torture other people. My days are filled with keeping Nina in line and watching over Gabriella so Lex doesn't stroke out when she plays at going up and down stairs. The usual."

"I know. It's just I'm so happy, I want it for you. I know it'll come when it's meant to and all that mystical stuff but I remember waiting. I remember wanting. I… well, I think it sucks you and Jack aren't mates. Or any of my wolves. I'd love to have you at Pacific with me. This having a baby thing is sort of scary. My mother-in-law is nice and all and with Ben's kids living with us, it's wonderful and I feel like I'm a mom already, but I want you. I want Mom."

Megan moved to lie beside Tracy and her sister put her head on Megan's shoulder with a soft, contented sound. The contact eased her frustration and they both relaxed.

"Portland isn't that far. I can be down there in three hours. All you have to do is ask. You know that, right? I love you." Megan's heart squeezed. For all Tracy's tough talk, it was Megan who was still surrounded by the Pack they grew up in while Tracy was in Portland with her new family.

Tracy sniffled. "I know. I'm just a bit weepy. The hormones are insane. I do love how Nick and Gabe just agree to whatever I demand though. That's some heady power tripping." Her sniffle morphed into a giggle and they both started laughing.

"Oh man. Cade baking cookies when his daughter needs a haircut, Lex popping a vein when Gabby decides it's super cool to jump from the middle of the stairs down to the bottom floor. Sid is the coolest dad ever and lets the kids take over his studio to make giant art projects and Layla, the most uptight woman I'd ever known before Sid, is all laid-back when her daughter has blue paint stains in her hair for a week. And now you guys. It's so cool. Tegan and Ben are trying. It's me and Dave now and he's totally abandoning me when Mom starts sniffing around. Believe you me, if Jack was my mate, I'd have nailed him ten times a day since we first met. Alas, nothing." She shrugged. "I'm not pining. I'm super busy. It is what it is. I can't change it. My life is really good except for the non-mate part. I date. I have sex. I have a great, albeit nosy family, a wonderful job." She exhaled sharply. "Aside from the really insane idea of a road trip to LA with my mother to a wedding, I'm happy."

And it was true, Megan reflected the next morning as she'd shuffled into the car, a giant cup of coffee in one hand and a huge bagel stuffed with ten kinds of protein in the other. She was happy. It wasn't something she thought about really. Some wolves were lucky enough to find mates early on. And others faced the horrible fate of losing them like Tegan had. It would happen when it happened so Megan thought it was utterly pointless to worry about it. It wasn't who she was anyway.

By the time they pulled up to the front of the swanky resort/hotel the wedding would be held in, Megan was ready to pull her hair out. Or shove someone out an air lock. Take your pick.

"Hey, hold your horses!" Tegan said as Megan got out even before she'd put the car into Park.

"I need to stretch my legs." She wanted to grab her suitcase, get into her swimsuit and sit out by the pool. Things had been good in werewolf politics in the two years since Cade had taken over National. No drama. No civil war. Megan was sure something would happen again, it always did, but it'd been some time since she'd had an actual vacation so it would be nice to have a little leisure.

Still she couldn't just abandon her grandmother in order to race to the registration desk. So she grabbed her grandmother's suitcase as well as her own and held her arm out.

"For a girl so fond of all the worst cuss words, you're a good granddaughter." Lia Warden smiled at Megan, mischief in her eyes.

"I think I've heard you use a few in your time." Megan winked and her grandmother laughed.

The check-in process should have been quick. So of course it wasn't. Her second cousin Sherry came squealing around the corner along with her mother who squealed equally loud and enveloped their mother into a hug. A three-person, hopping, squealing unit that made Megan cringe and back slowly away.

"What the fuck is that?" Nina murmured.

"Why hello, Alpha Warden!" Megan smirked as a plan began to hatch. "That's cousin Sherry, the bride to be, and her mom. Nancy is my mom's favorite cousin. There are six sisters and they're all just like Nancy only Nancy is the calmest one."

Nina's eyebrows rose in alarm and Megan laughed. "You're shitting me?"

"I told you it was going to be like chewing tinfoil. I told you we should have flown. But does anyone listen to me? Nope. And you're the Alpha so get on over there and start squealing too." Megan shoved her and Nina sent her a look of alarmed murderous intent as Beth caught her arm and dragged her into the melee.

"Dude, she's going to get you for that." Tegan sidled up to her side, chuckling. "Still, it'll be worth it just to remember that look on her face. Over and over again. Do you think she'd notice if I took a picture with my phone?"

Megan had the camera out already. "Well, it's a wedding. We need pictures don't you think?"

Grace approached. "I saved you at the restaurant last night," she said quickly.

"So you did." Megan snapped a few pictures of Nina smushed up against several women wearing blouses with at least two dozen pieces of flair on them. She hoped she could find a way to work it into the conversation that Nina needed one just like it. Payment would be steep so she had to make it worth the retribution Nina would heap on her head.

Nina's eyes flashed as the camera did and the other Warden women who'd stayed in the background burst out laughing.

"I'm going to get checked in so we can get the bags squared away," Megan announced as she quickly stopped at the throng, kissing and hugging everyone. She didn't even wince when Nina pinched her side.

Thankfully, her grandmother seemed to want to get

away from all the noise so Megan helped her to her room with her bags.

Once she got her grandmother settled, she turned to leave but Lia Warden wasn't ready for her to go just yet.

"Megan, darling, I've been thinking about you a lot lately."

Uh oh. She turned and smiled but her grandmother had that faraway look in her eyes she got when something witchy was brewing in her head. And the thing of it was, as much as they all made light of her grandmother's little pronouncements, she was always right. Damned spooky.

"Is that so? Should I be worried?"

"Well, big things for you. All of my grandchildren are destined for greatness. But none of you has had an easy path. I wish I could say I thought it would be different for you. But I don't. You have a trial ahead. I don't know if the ending will be something you want or not." Her grandmother cocked her head and touched Megan's cheek. "But you're strong. Your heart is full and you know to count on your family and who you are."

"Is this about a dude or politics or what?"

Her grandmother shrugged and then leaned in to kiss Megan's cheek. "I never know. I didn't know about Nina, just that her brother would get killed. I sensed Pellini but not Grace. Could be your mate, could be something else. You'll be ready for it. I know you will. You're my girl."

With that, she was dismissed as her grandmother turned on the television and exclaimed when she saw it was an episode of *Law and Order*. Once Jerry Orbach was on the screen, Megan knew she'd been forgotten so she waved absently, called out her thanks and an I love you, and let herself out.

Despite her grandmother's little talk, Megan was free. Blessedly so for the first time in a few days and that in and of itself was cause for happiness. She quickly got herself to her room, sighing happily after she closed the door and began to root through her suitcase for her swimsuit.

But of course ten minutes after she'd ensconced herself in the sun, a cool iced tea at the ready, her iPod working and her sunglasses shading her eyes, her mother showed up.

"Megan, we need an extra set of hands. We're stuffing the favors for the tables. Well, don't you look nice? My goodness that's a very sexy swimsuit."

With a sigh and a bit of a cringe at her mother saying her suit was sexy, she heaved herself up from her lounger. She barely had time to yank her cover-up on as her mother dragged her over to the big table just across the pool area where she saw the rest of her family had gathered.

"Okay, I'll give you a freebie because, as Dave reminded me, I did give you a hard time just last month with Lex." Nina looked so magnanimous when she said it Megan snorted.

"I let your ass go off to the garden show with just one guard and then you got your butt hauled in to the station house because you started arguing with a cop. Lex yelled at me for twenty minutes."

Nina snickered. "Yeah, like I said. But don't abandon me again."

"Whatever. I got years of freebies after being your guard. Don't forget it the next time I need a favor."

She really got a look at the table and suddenly wished for those hours back in the car on the way south. Piles and piles of neatly cut squares of… "What is this?"

"Tulle! Isn't it precious? It matches my bridesmaids' dresses perfectly! You see how I've got three shades of purple?" Sherry actually giggled and Megan had a few uncharitable thoughts about her cousin and her predilection to speaking in exclamation points.

"So you take this cashew mix, and isn't that clever? Because you know everyone else does Jordan almonds but we did cashew mix with a little bit of sugar on the outside!" Sherry's mother had the same giggle. "And you put three or four pieces here in the center and then tie it in a bow like this." Nancy made quick work of the little packet and put it aside. "Just be sure to use the ribbon that coordinates with the tulle."

And so began three hours of stuffing nuts into tiny squares of differently hued purple net. Three hours. Even Layla began to get cranky after hour two.

Finally they broke for dinner and headed back to their rooms to get changed.

Nina's and Megan's rooms adjoined so Nina threw the connecting door open and then dramatically fell on Megan's bed with a howl. "Oh my God. Seriously? Your mother is insane. She enjoyed that. Every minute of fucking ribbon talk and she got a spoon and ate it up. I'm officially brain-dead."

Megan laughed as she swiped some lip gloss on and zipped the side of her dress. "And you thought she was on you to have kids before you finally ponied up and had Gabby. At least you didn't have to go through this to get married."

"Yes well, I nearly died and all, which sort of gives

me a get-out-of-tulle-free card." Nina rolled over and sat up.

"Whatever. You can't live off that one forever. You're like the queen of the Pack now so stop whining. Anyway, you snuck off four or five times to call home. And by the way, calling home does not include hanging out having ice cream on the other side of the pool. If you're going to skive off, at least hide it better."

Nina wandered into her room grumbling and returned some moments later, yanking a dress on and turning her back to Megan. "Zip me, sister."

Megan zipped the dress and swatted Nina's rear. "Zipped. And you know? I mean, silly tulle and twelve shades of purple aside, she was totally happy to be getting married. That's pretty cool even if she works my nerves. You should be that excited to be uniting your life with your partner. Sure, sure, in a less annoying fashion would be my preference, but when I finally sniff out Mr. Right, I'd like to be that flipping into it."

Nina smiled. "Yeah, you're right. But if we have to do anything like that tomorrow I'm faking appendicitis. Do werewolves have appendicitis?"

Megan laughed as they left to meet the rest of the group for dinner.

After the three-hour dinner where yet more exclamation-point-littered conversation about tulle and purple ribbon took up nearly every last bit of oxygen, Megan escaped and fell into bed, exhausted.

At least she'd managed to have a quiet word with Tee about heading off for shooting and shoes, two of their favorite things. They hadn't schemed together like that in a while, so that had made her heart lighter.

Visions of targets and the perfect pair of heels danced in her head as she finally dropped off to sleep.

But she should have known it was too good to be true.

As she and Tegan quickly and quietly made their way down the back stairwell and through the side of the lobby to escape for their day of freedom, they halted at the sight of their mother blocking the doors.

"There you girls are! You two look so pretty today. It's funny," she said, grabbing them both and turning them away from freedom and leading them back toward the interior of the hotel, "you two look so much alike when you're together trying to outmaneuver me like you did when you were little. You weren't leaving were you? Because Layla is over with the groom's mother and sister at the fitting and I just caught Nina and sent her to go ride along with Sherry to take one last look at the flowers. Isn't it nice we had an expert? And Tracy is sleeping in this morning, she says she's not well after the trip, poor dear. But you two and Grace can help with errands."

Tegan looked over the top of their mother's head at Megan and they both rolled their eyes. It'd been a long time since the two of them teamed up to outwit their mother and it'd been fun while it lasted. At least she wasn't off with Sherry looking at roses like Nina was.

Chapter Two

Well, at least she wasn't tying bows to chairs.

Instead she sat in the bar at LAX, sipping a club soda with lime, absently watching a baseball game on the big screen across the room. Her mother had sent her to pick up a relative from the groom's side, who also happened to be Layla's Anchor, Shane Rosario.

Shane the doctor. Shane the purported pretty boy who practiced medicine in Las Vegas and lived like a human, outside a Pack. Which was why she'd never met him. In a culture where an Anchor was like a member of your family, it was common for Anchors to spend good chunks of time with the pair he was bonded with.

But not Shane. Aside from the one weekend he'd come up from medical school over a decade before to perform the tri-bond with Layla, he'd not ever been to Cascadia territory. He'd met her family once and Megan had been away on a high school ski trip and wasn't there. Tracy talked about him for years afterward though.

Lay and Sid traveled to Vegas at least twice a year to see him and they often emailed and spoke on the phone but he didn't have a close relationship with the kids.

Frankly, Megan thought it was strange and sort of offensive. But Layla defended him, saying he was raised to be suspicious of werewolf culture by his mother who'd never made the change from human to werewolf. What sort of mindfuck would it be to be raised by someone who hated what you were? She couldn't even begin to imagine.

And in the end, what difference did it make? If it was all right with Sid and Layla, her feelings were irrelevant.

Shane hefted his overnight bag and headed toward baggage claim. The plane had arrived early so he'd just get his suitcase and call Layla to let her know he was there. She was probably here already anyway. He smiled, thinking about her. If it weren't for her presence at this wedding he'd have never agreed to come.

As it was, his paternal aunts would be there and would pester him relentlessly about when he planned to settle down and live within a Pack. His father had given up years before and Shane ignored the twinge of pain he knew he'd caused by his rejection of half his racial identity.

He was doing just fine in Las Vegas. He dated human women and one day he'd find one he liked enough to marry and then they'd adopt children. He didn't want to raise a child like he was, part of something he didn't understand or want to accept. He shuddered to think how his mother would react anyway.

Once he'd exited the security area, he passed by a small bar. The Dodgers game on the big screen caught his attention first, but nearly immediately he stopped dead in his tracks at the sight of the honeyed blonde sitting alone, sipping her drink. Slow green eyes, heavy

lidded but sharp, slid from the game to his face and rec-
ognition hit, holding him rooted to the spot.

Her otherness radiated from her body. She wasn't
human but her smile, the way one corner of her mouth
tilted up like the curve of a waist, was more than reason enough to overlook it. He was in Los Angeles after
all, loads of shifters in the Southland.

He ambled over and she cocked her head as she
leaned back and pushed the chair opposite hers out with
a prettily sandaled foot.

"Hi there." He grinned.

The scent of the lime in her soda water tickled his
nose. But it was her elemental scent that made his hormones sit up and take notice. She smelled like honey
and heady flowers.

She tucked her hair behind an ear and simple gold
hoops winked in the low light. "Hi yourself."

"So the story goes like this," he said, leaning in to
take a deep whiff of her and liking it. A lot. "Here I
am, dreading seeing a bunch of relatives and I walk past
and see you. The sight of those green eyes of yours just
made my day a lot better."

God he was usually way smoother than this but she
made him feel sort of giddy. Stupid with wanting to
touch her.

She laughed. "My goodness, I bet you say that to all
the werewolves you meet in airport bars." Her graceful
hands fiddled with her napkin, shredding it into long
strips and then balling the strips up. Over and over. Silly
but it mesmerized him.

He figured Layla would forgive him for being late if
he stayed and chatted this lovely lady up for a bit longer.

His plane would only be arriving just now anyway, he thought as he checked his watch.

That's when she checked her watch and swore softly. "I'm sorry. I'm picking someone up. I need to get to baggage claim. If I lose him, my sister will kill me."

He nearly lost his mind when she stood. Her waist was so close he could have leaned in and brushed his lips against her belly. He smelled her, the heat of her skin, the full-on spice of her arousal. Licking his lips to try and get himself under control, he thought hard and realized what she'd said.

"Wait." He stood. "This is so weird. I'm Shane Rosario. I should have recognized those beautiful eyes. You're one of Layla's sisters, right?"

She took a step back and a wall slammed between them suddenly. "Oh." She heaved a breath. "Yes. Of course. I'm Megan. Nice to meet you. Shall we go get your bags then? I know Layla can't wait to see you."

She hurried past as he tried to figure out what exactly had happened. Had Layla been angry with him and said something negative to her sister? Is that why she wasn't there to pick him up herself?

Scrambling to catch up with the younger and ever-so-fetching Warden sister, he took a moment to admire the long legs and the high, tight ass. A shocking vision nearly felled him. A vision of his fingers digging into that muscle as he fucked deep into her body, the sheen of sweat on her bare skin making her glow like moonlight.

Of course he was Layla's Anchor. Why not? The first hot-looking werewolf who'd come on to her when she was pretty open to random sexing to take her mind off ribbon-and-tulle squares and he's her sister's man. Well, sort of. Enough sort of to invoke the sister rule.

Funny how she'd felt this total connection with him right off too. Probably the anchor connection he had to her sister. She wanted to fuck the hell out of Jack Meyers too and he was Grace's Anchor. Maybe that was it.

She just needed to get his luggage and haul his ass back to the hotel so he could hang out with Layla while Megan avoided him the best she could until they returned to Seattle on Sunday.

My goodness, though, but he was big. Big and brawny and really masculine. Just the way she liked her men. When a woman was five-eight, it was hard to find a man who filled that secret little thrill spot. Megan was a tough person, hard in a lot of ways, she could handle just about any physical threat and it was her job to do so. But it would be so nice to have a man who could take charge, make her feel cosseted from time to time.

She sighed and his long strides ate up the ground until he'd caught up with her. "I was expecting to see Layla. Is she all right?"

Oh now that was just rich, wasn't it? Megan held her annoyance in check, barely, as they rounded the corner and headed toward the baggage area for his flight.

"Sorry, you're stuck with me for your ride. She's been dealing with the groom's family today, taking them places, all that stuff. Everyone was shorthanded so I got sent to pick you up." She knew the smile she sent his way was tight when he winced a bit.

"God, I'm really fucking this up. You're mad and I didn't…it wasn't my intention to insult you. I was just curious about Lay. Believe me, it's no chore to be picked up from the airport by a woman with legs as long as yours."

His grin was sexy too. She saw a bit of Sid in his face, not so surprising as they were cousins after all. He had the same black hair, the olive complexion. His eyes brown, not extraordinarily so, but they were big and nice. The dimple she saw when he grinned, just to the side of his mouth was positively delicious.

"You'll see Lay at the hotel. She's excited you're coming." She turned back to the conveyor belt and he grabbed his suitcase and turned back her way.

"Okay, ready."

He had no idea what the hell was going on but that question about Layla had pushed her away even further. Gone was the sexy, flirty smile she'd gifted him with in the bar, replaced by a cool distance.

Damned if his ridiculous need to touch her still wasn't there, though. He didn't want her to be upset with him. He certainly didn't want her thinking he was an asshole. If for no other reason than she was Layla's sister, he wanted to get along with her. But he liked Megan Warden. Liked the way she prowled as she walked.

She was a woman totally at home in her skin and he envied it. Envied the ease with which she wore her otherness. It was sexy, exciting, incredibly enticing.

On the way back to the car he kept close. "So do you just think I'm an asshole or what?"

She stopped at a huge SUV and clicked the locks open. "No. Why would you say that?"

He loaded his bags in and walked around to get inside. Once he'd shut the door, the sound of the world

died away, the scents of asphalt and smog withered, and
suddenly he was hyperaware of her.

His gaze was locked with hers, he watched, fascinated as her pupils swallowed the sea of green. His
breath seized as he truly scented her. Honey, lilacs,
something else…

"Oh. Well then."

He swallowed hard, trying to figure out what she
meant. "What?" And then he knew. Understood. Despite the fact he'd lived his life outside a Pack, pretty
much as a human, he did understand the mate bond.
Believed in its power and knew she has his. Surety
settled into his system even as he itched to rub himself
all over her skin to mark her in some way. He'd only
felt this much werewolf a few times in his life. When
he first changed and when he performed the tri-bond
with Layla and Sid. It freaked him out, the wolf under
his skin, the one his mother taught him to fear. But at
the same time, the downright *rightness* of what he felt
for her, of what he knew the mate bond to be, overruled
his fear. He would have her, he would seal the bond and
celebrate that part of himself. Tomorrow he'd worry
about the rest.

He could barely hold a thought as need held him in
her grip. "Go. How far is it?"

She jammed the key into the ignition one handed
as she buckled up with the other. "Twenty minutes.
Pray for light traffic. Get money out for the ticket. In
the console."

He fumbled with the console and finally just yanked
his wallet out to pay for parking. Of course there was
a huge back up to pay but eventually they got through
and she headed for the freeway.

* * *

He placed his hand on her thigh and the hem of her skirt rose as his fingers inched it upward enough that he could touch bare skin.

Megan gasped, never having felt anything with such total electric sensation before. She gripped the wheel so hard her bones creaked at the strain. She had to concentrate on driving but all she wanted to do was lick him up one side and down the other.

She remembered Tracy and Nick that first day they'd met and how Tracy had just been swept away by the bond and her need to be with him. Megan hadn't been able to grasp what that sort of need would be like. Until then, she tried not to get pulled over for speeding as she raced back toward the hotel.

If anyone stopped them when they arrived, she'd probably throw down with them. Best not to think on it. Best to just try and focus on driving. She wanted to talk to him, to learn more about him but she didn't have the mental ability to concentrate on speaking, driving and not jumping those utterly delectable bones of his.

"Nearly there? God, your skin is so soft." He stroked his fingertips along her upper thigh, sending shivers through her. His voice was rusty, like he hadn't used it in a long time.

"Two more exits. And we're going to crash if you keep that up. I can barely concentrate as it is."

His fingers stilled but he didn't remove his hand. He chuckled softly. "Gotcha."

Just seven minutes later, not that she'd been watching the clock on the dash or anything, she pulled into a space in the hotel garage.

"Your room. Don't let anyone stop you." Urgency

threaded through his voice, rode her hard as well as she scrabbled to get out.

"We'll take this side door, back through the pool area. They might be in the lobby."

He circled an arm around her waist, carrying his overnight bag but leaving his suitcase behind as they hustled toward the hotel.

Single-mindedly, she guided him through the area, scenting those she knew and avoiding them. They took the stairwell to her room and she barricaded her connecting door and put up the do not disturb sign, bolted the outer door and turned to face him.

Chapter Three

He could no longer hold on once they entered her room and she locked the door. His head swam in a sea of her scent. Of her desire, of the basic imprint of her on the room around him. He. Had. To. Claim. Her.

When she turned to face him, the primal male inside him thrilled to see her eyes widen at how close he stood to her. A soft sigh filtered from her mouth. A mouth he set his own to and fell.

Her taste roared through him. His senses hummed with satisfaction, his body hardened as his brain filled with all that was his woman. He wanted to consume her, wanted every inch of her inside and out. Never in his life had anyone ever held so much fascination for him and for the first time since he'd began to really struggle with who and what he was, he reveled in it. Accepted that he was a werewolf and she was his mate. The freedom of it was nearly as heady as the connection of their two hearts and souls.

Her head fell against the door as he pulled the front of her pretty dress open, the muted sounds of buttons flying and pinging off the carpet and walls filling the space between heaving breaths. Beneath was a feast for his eyes. Acres of creamy skin. A flat belly. Pretty dark blue panties and a matching bra.

Bending his head, he feasted on the smattering of freckles on the curve of her right breast as he popped the catch of her bra, freeing them into his grateful hands.

"Oh!" she exclaimed. "More. Touch me, Shane. Claim me."

She writhed against him and his body reacted as her scent filled him up to the bursting point. He wanted her with single-minded intensity.

"God. God. You're so fucking beautiful. I…" Instead of saying more he showed her. Cruised his mouth along her collarbone. Sturdy. Strong and yet totally feminine. He licked along the hollow of her throat, swallowing the frantic beat of her pulse, tasting the echo of his own need as it seeped from her skin.

Her nipples, so sensitive they beaded as he moved to them, tasted like everything he'd ever wanted and never knew he craved. Her arousal hung between them like something tangible. The scent held him, fascinated, enthralled. His cock throbbed along with the beat of her heart under his tongue as he licked up the line of her chest, up her neck, capturing her earlobe for just a brief moment until she cried out.

"Help me!"

With two moves, his pants were down. He kicked them free and she wrapped a long, muscular leg around his waist, drawing him tight to her. Her dress hung in tatters. He yanked off her panties, the sound of ripping silk doing things to him low and deep.

All he could think of was shoving his cock into her even as he knew he should take his time, show her pleasure.

"Inside or I will maim you," she gasped out and he obliged, guiding his cock to her gate. The slippery entrance bathed the head of his cock in wet heat.

He laughed, totally happy for the first time in his life, as he surged up and into her body with a cry of joy.

He stilled and she felt more than just his cock inside her, it was as if she'd cracked herself open and he'd settled within her. His joy ebbed into her very bones, married with hers. It was so right. Tears swam, blurring her vision. Her view of this man's face. His beautiful face.

It was then, her gaze locked with his, as he pressed back inside, she saw his wolf there, in his eyes. The loneliness of it struck her deep. This wolf of his wanted to be free, to be loved and she knew then, knew as she knew he was hers, their road would not be easy.

"Your wolf is so beautiful," she said softly. Despite that knowing, she knew she wanted him forever and would fight for him too. For that moment, she would revel in what they had because it was beautiful.

His breath caught and he shook his head. "Wrap your legs around me." His hands, big and strong, cradled her naked ass as he fucked her up against the door. Urgency marred his features, the line of his mouth was hard as she leaned forward to kiss it.

He opened to her, kissing her back as she held on, her fingers digging into his shoulders. She wanted his bare skin, needed it, so she ripped off his shirt, reveling in the way his intake of breath echoed into their kiss.

She let herself wonder in the feel of his body, in the way his skin tautened over the bunch and play of his muscles as he thrust into her body. Broad shoulders beckoned and she gave in, leaving his mouth to press her lips into the dip just below his collarbone.

His cock was fat, broad and wide like his shoulders, a big man all around and she couldn't wait to see him totally naked and spread out on the bed so she could touch and taste every part of him.

"I'm not going to last much longer," he managed to gasp out, "it's so intense being inside you. Beautiful."

She smiled and nipped his biceps just above where the sleeve of his shirt hung from his arm.

"So come. Come inside me and mark me as yours."

"Christ." He rested his forehead on her shoulder a moment, still fucking into her body. "You're irresistible, you know that? And mine. What a lucky man I am. Make yourself come, my hands are filled with your ass just now."

She laughed, arching her body a bit to make some space to move her fingers to her clit. "I'll warn you, I like to come. A lot. I like sex and I'm very exacting." She hummed as the pleasure of her fingertips sliding against her clit added to the feel of his cock stretching her, filling her, stroking inside.

"Well, lucky for me then."

He may have started to say more but she lost all ability to hear anything but the rush in her ears as she started to climax and a deep, rumbling growl came from his gut as he joined her.

He filled her, sealing the bond between them and she barely felt it when he fell to his knees, shielding her from the impact of it, holding her against him as he pressed lips to her temple.

He rushed into her senses, disorienting her a moment when she opened her eyes and saw double, felt double, but after some sweaty minutes, her heartbeat began to slow to normal and she looked into his face, caught his smile.

Shane knew he'd found something more special than he could wrap his brain around as he held Megan against his body. So perfect. Strong. Gorgeous.

"Hi there." He kissed her forehead and stood, helping her to her feet. She ran inside him like the blood in his veins and while at first it had felt strange, unnatural, by then it just felt right.

"Hi yourself." She grinned. "So um, wow. Here we are all post-coital and I don't even know your birthday."

They didn't know each other very well at all and the reality of their situation began to hit him. Still, he couldn't be sorry for finding her. Regardless of his choice to live outside a Pack, he accepted certain things about himself. He was a werewolf and he saw the bond between his parents. Even if his mother rejected the wolf half of his father, she loved him and he adored her. So much his father had lived outside a pack because his mother had hated it so much. So he knew it was real even if it wasn't perfect. The love was there between them, enough that his father had given up his wolf half and his mother had stayed even though she had been uncomfortable with that part of him.

With Layla and Sid, he saw two mates, two wolves who accepted each other wholly and completely. They had children together, had created a family and a life. Hell, as Layla's Anchor, he was part of that himself and that feeling of belonging to something bigger than himself was something he treasured.

"We have time. It's March fourth by the way. Now, a

shower beckons I think. I want to see you totally naked. In exchange, I'll make you come again."

She shrugged off the remains of her dress and let the bra fall to her feet. He'd already tossed her panties somewhere over his shoulder. Gloriously naked, tall, hard and fit, she was the sexiest thing he'd ever seen.

"I have to tell you those are the finest breasts I've ever clapped eyes on." He tugged her toward the bathroom.

"As much as I'm totally all over that idea, especially since it involves us both naked and having more sex, my phone has been ringing and I'd wager yours has too. Everyone is going to be wondering where we are."

He scrubbed his hands over his face. "I don't care. I want you and those three minutes against the door were not enough. God knows I don't want you to think that's the game I'm bringing."

She laughed and kissed him. "I'm perfectly willing to give you a second chance. That was claiming, I'm sure with that body of yours and that very fine cock, you've got an A game in there."

He wrapped his arms around her, quite liking the feel of her against him and unable to remember any other woman. It was as if she'd totally pushed all memories from his head. He couldn't decide if he should be happy or distressed by this point. He was seeing a woman back in Vegas and obviously that was over.

"I don't want to leave. I want to stay in here with you for a few days."

"I can feel you, you know. You're panicking."

She pushed him back.

"Not that. It just occurred to me there's a lot of stuff to be resolved. Neither of us was expecting this obviously." He saw the disbelief on her face, felt her unhappiness and wanted to fix it. "Hey, I was also thinking about how much I loved the way you felt in my arms and that you'd erased the memory of all other women."

She snorted but the rigidity in her spine eased.

To underline her point, right as he'd moved his lips back to her nipple, his phone rang from the pocket of his overnight bag near the door. Layla's ring—Eric Clapton.

"My sister obviously." She pushed him back as she said it. "Go on. Tell her we'll meet her downstairs in the pool area in five minutes. Don't tell her about the bond or we'll have two dozen wolves pounding on the door."

Before he could answer, she'd turned and gone into the bathroom, shutting the door in his face.

He grabbed his phone while struggling into the T-shirt he was thankful to have tossed into his carry-on that morning. "Hey there."

"Where are you? I saw the car in the lot when I came back from this hellish day of errands. Please tell me Megan didn't strand you at the airport, she's usually really on top of things."

He smiled at the very idea. "I'm really good actually. I have a lot to tell you. I'm here at the hotel. Megan said to tell you we'd meet you in the pool area in five minutes."

"Okay we'll sneak off for dinner."

He hesitated. He wanted to see Layla. He loved her, she was his Anchor but Megan was his mate. Any plans he made would involve her and while he wasn't a woman, he certainly knew them well enough to understand there'd most likely be some jealousy between them until Megan understood she was first with him.

"We'll see you in a few." He hung up before she could say anything else.

* * *

Megan looked at herself in the mirror with a sigh. All her life she'd been a pretty confident person. Except when it came to Layla. Layla was the smartest sibling. Certainly Layla and Tegan gave each other some hefty competition when it came to beauty but they were the ones who got the best boobs and the red hair. And after Tegan had lost Lucas, Tegan had gotten a lot closer to Layla than to Megan. It had hurt. She loved her sisters, every one of them, but they were hard on a woman's confidence sometimes.

And Layla had him first. She *knew* it was stupid to feel jealous but she did. It wasn't like Shane had done anything and she knew Lay would never in a million years betray Shane or hurt Megan. But it was there anyway. Layla was someone really special to Shane and she'd been that way to him first.

Of course she had no clothes in the bathroom so she cleaned up quickly, applying some eyeliner and lipstick before heading back out to the room.

"Now I really don't want to go anywhere." He looked her up and down slowly, approval clear in his gaze.

"You can go on down if you want. Meet up with me later." She pulled on underwear and a skirt before turning to grab a bra and look for a shirt.

He was there, touching her before she could take another step. "Why would I want that? I want to be with you, Megan."

"I just meant, well, I know you've been looking forward to seeing Layla and she's been talking about you for weeks so I didn't want to get in the way or anything."

He wouldn't let her move away to put her shirt on, instead holding her to him and breathing in deeply at her neck. "Of course I want to see Layla. But you can be there too, right? She's always given me the impression you were close."

"She has? I mean, sure. I like all my siblings, even my brothers who will of course grill you and try to intimidate you and stuff. Just ignore them."

She wriggled enough until he let her go so she could get her shirt on.

He groaned as they walked out of the room. He didn't want to go anywhere but back inside where he could get her naked and treat her the way she was meant to be treated. That quickie earlier wasn't enough.

Her feet, my God, her toes were deep red in the daintiest sandals. It seemed totally at odds with the tough Enforcer Layla had always spoken about.

"You have the sexiest, longest legs," he murmured as he kept her close with an arm around her waist. He still smelled her on his skin and never wanted to lose that feeling.

She actually blushed. "Oh, well, thank you. I run ten miles a day, I think that probably helps."

When the elevator doors opened and they walked out onto the patio area surrounding two large pools, Layla launched herself at him with a happy laugh, dropping kisses on his cheeks. He laughed, hugging her back, happy as hell to see her.

Megan stepped away and more than her physical distance, he felt her emotional distance like a slap.

He set Layla away from him, no easy feat because she'd been hugging him, but before he could turn to Megan, Layla gasped.

"Oh! You're mated! That's the best news ever. Congratulations." She turned and began to yell that Megan and Shane were mated and people started to rush over.

Megan smiled dutifully at her mother and he noted her twin, Tegan, coming over to hug her sister too. He wanted to touch her, to reassure her, but she'd been swallowed in a sea of female wolves talking excitedly. It was a wedding they were all there for, he supposed, and that had to add to the thrill of a new mating.

He saw some of his male relatives and relief fell over him as Adam, a cousin of his and Sid's showed up.

"Hey, congratulations. Megan is a really special woman. You're a lucky man to have her."

Shane couldn't have agreed more. But he had something he needed to discuss with Adam in private as well.

Megan felt Shane's happiness at seeing Layla and wanted to kick him and punch her sister. Cripes this was stupid. Couldn't she find a guy like Sid who wanted her that much?

Pissed off now, at herself for being pissed off as much as at them, all she wanted to do was escape and try to deal with her rampant emotions, but her mother had an iron grip on her arm as she busily began to plan a double wedding with Sherry.

"No. Mom, this is Sherry's day and I don't want to encroach on that. I need to go call Lex. I'll be back. He'll be mad at us for not calling right off."

"Oh you're right. We'll all go to dinner tonight then. I don't know Shane as well as I'd like. Where are you going to live? Surely not Packless in Las Vegas of all places?"

"I don't know. We just met less than three hours ago.

I'll be back." She indicated her phone, and her mother let go so Megan made a hasty escape.

Reality replaced the haze of the new mate bond. God this sucked. Where would they live? Because her mother was right, she wouldn't go Packless, give up her career and her life in Seattle to pretend to be human three states away. She was a werewolf. She ran as a wolf every day if she could. Maybe he'd want to live in Seattle, want to try a life with a big family. They had a lot of talking to do.

Instead of going back to her room, she headed to the gardens in the resort to find a place to call Lex and to think over her situation.

Lex answered on the first ring. "Hi, hon. Is everything okay?"

"I met my mate today. It's Shane, Layla's anchor bond and he had sex with her and I'm never going to be able to forget it and how can I? She's got bigger boobs and he lives in Las Vegas without a Pack and he probably wishes he was mated to her instead of me." She was pretty sure she didn't even take a breath during all of that but she just needed to say it and he'd understand.

And he did. "Aw, Megan, gorgeous, of course he wants you as his mate. You're just nervous and I can see why although I try not to ever imagine you or any of my sisters having sex. He is your mate. Period. What you feel for your Anchor is special, yes, but you know as well as I do, it's not the same as a mate bond. Cade does not feel for Nina what he feels for Grace. I imagine it'll be hard but you'll get through it. As for him being Packless, honey, is that what you want? Are you sure you can be happy that way?"

No she couldn't. A werewolf was meant to live in a

community with other wolves. They survived, thrived, through touch and being with those in their family. It was part of who they were. She saw Shane's wolf and she never wanted that, not for herself and not even for him.

"No. I'm Enforcer of Cascadia. It's not just what I do, it's what I was born to be, part of me. I'm hoping he'll want to come up to live in Seattle. We haven't talked about it yet. Right now Layla is rubbing herself all over him and he's surrounded by Wardens."

"She's not rubbing herself all over him. Lay would not do that to you. Hell or to Sid. Go back and face him. Talk to him. Tell him if he hurts you I'll be forced to kill him. I love you and I'm so happy for you. Shall I come down? Gabby and I can be on a plane in a few hours."

"No. He and I need time alone, away from family to try and work all this stuff through. I love you, Lex."

He chuckled softly and Megan heard Gabby talking like a monkey on the other end. "I love you too, Megan. Everything is going to be all right. The bond will guide you and get you guys through."

"Where the hell have you been?"

Sometime later, Tegan, Tracy, Nina, Grace and Layla all burst through the wrought iron gate and into the garden.

"What's it to you? Not like you noticed I was even there." How dare Layla give her attitude!

"What? I turned around to congratulate you and you were gone. Mom said you were coming right back so we waited but you never came back. Shane is looking for you."

"Why are you here?"

"What is up your ass?" Layla narrowed her eyes at her sister, who narrowed them right back.

"You're up my ass. Rubbing yourself all over Shane. You're married! And he's *mine*." God she sounded like such a bitch.

Grace sat down on the bench and pulled Megan down beside her. "You, over there and shut up for a minute." She pointed to Layla who started to argue but Tracy and Nina pulled her back. Tegan sat next to Megan with a sigh, putting her head on Megan's shoulder.

"Oh, honey, I know where you are right now." Grace looked over at Nina who nodded back at her. "When I met Nina and she was such an insufferable cow, it was horrible. I knew Cade cared about her and I could see how much she cared about him. It sucked."

"I was pregnant and you just pranced into my house all tiny and cute. Who wouldn't hate you?" Nina snorted and Grace laughed.

"I am tiny and cute, aren't I?"

Megan laughed at their back and forth. They were so close, despite the distance.

"You can't think I'd ever do anything with Shane? Even if you weren't his mate, I'd never do that. I'm hurt you have such a low opinion of me, Megan." Damn if Layla didn't still look gorgeous even as she was angry.

"I don't care. I'm sorry, Lay, but I don't care if you're hurt. You fucked my mate. He's seen you naked. He loved you before me. That sucks. It sucks and I can't apologize for it. It's always about you, damn it. Oh poor Layla with her hurt feelings. Well, let me make you feel better. You have a man who adores you. Who didn't even flinch to move his entire life to Seattle to be with you. I have a man who adores *you* and who I doubt will

want to move to Seattle and I am *Second* of the Pack
and I really get the feeling my mate, a man who could
move, isn't going to want to. So fuck you, Layla. Okay?
That makes me petty and small but I just don't care."

She got up and Lay did too as everyone watched
carefully. "You're acting like a spoiled brat. He's lived
outside a Pack his whole life. He's been raised to be
suspicious of what we are. Of what he is. His mother
has done a number on him, let me tell you. The first
time he changed she punished him! She's raised him
to think his wolf is unnatural and wrong and his father
loves her so much, so much he's simply let Shane be
estranged from what he is. This is going to be hard on
him. You're not even giving him a chance."

Rage and humiliation coursed through Megan.
Disbelief that any mother would do that. But it didn't
overcome everything else. "You're acting like a self-
righteous bitch. Why is this about him? You should be
thinking about me. But you're not because Layla is the
center of Layla world. Oh how dare I not be available
when you decided you wanted to congratulate me. Poor
Shane, my goodness let's not let him feel bad. Gosh
between you and your fucking feelings and Shane and
his fucking feelings you might not even remember who
he's mated to. I'm sure he's having a hard time with it."

"You both need to be smacked. Megan, honey, you
know I adore the hell out of you, but you're jumping to
conclusions about Shane, aren't you? And you, Layla,
come on, how would you feel if your sister had slept
with Sid and had an anchor connection to her? Of course
she's upset. Both of you, knock this shit off right now
before you say something you can't take back." Nina
stood and got between them.

"I don't care. Smack me. I know enough to have felt his emotions once we completed the bond. He's panicked about me but *thrilled* when she rubbed herself all over him. Is it too much to ask that I get a mate who adores me the way your men adore you? I've been patient! Each one of you has found someone and I never begrudged that. I was genuinely happy when you found them. It's bad enough I have to live in the shadow of Miss Gorgeous Perfect over there and now I get her sloppy seconds. Lucky me." Megan knew she was losing it but she couldn't seem to stop saying it.

"Perfect? Oh my God! Megan, look at yourself, you goddamned overachiever. You're Second in our Pack. You're the youngest female to ever hold such a powerful spot."

"By two minutes," Tegan said, trying to break the tension. She was Second in the Great Lakes Pack.

Layla waved it away. "You're kick-ass and super smart and you're blonde and you have those damned arms like Linda Hamilton did in *The Terminator*, the second one where she was all nutty and tried to kill the doctor with a pen. Right about now that's reminding me of you too. You don't have breasts that've fed two kids. I can't believe you'd be jealous of me. That's the dumbest thing I've ever heard." She grabbed Megan's arms and gave her a little shake. "I love you. I would never do anything to hurt you purposely. You or Sid or the kids, the Pack, or Shane for that matter. I hate that you'd think so little of me."

Megan slumped, hating that she would too.

"I'm sorry."

Layla started crying and hugged her. "I'm sorry too.

This should be a happy day for you. I know he's happy to have found you. I know you guys can make it work."

"I'm scared." Damn it, she was. Even if she hated to say it out loud. Her sisters surrounded her again. "What if we can't make it work? What if I'm not enough?"

"You're his mate, Megan. You're enough simply by existing. But more than that, look at yourself. He's so lucky to have you. You will fight for him and be the best thing that ever happened to him." Layla sniffled as she said it and Megan had no doubt her sister meant every word. Even if she wasn't sure she believed it herself.

Shane had been talking to Adam about serving as their Anchor when Megan's anguish swept through their bond and nearly felled him. Urgency made his heart pound. He had to help her.

This bond thing came with a lot of stuff he hadn't really thought out, wasn't sure he wanted it but it was too late. He was all bound up in her and she with him. It was good, he liked it even as he resented it. Way down deep he struggled with what he'd been taught and what he felt.

"Shane, are you all right?" Adam looked concerned.

"I am. This is all new. I don't quite know how to process it." He looked around, worried, but she wasn't anywhere in view. Neither were any of her sisters. Maybe he'd just give her a call to check in.

He pulled out his phone but realized he didn't even have her number. "I don't have her number." He looked back to Adam. "Have you seen Megan?"

"Not since we started talking. Is everything okay with her? Can you feel something through the bond?"

"I'll call Lay, she probably knows where Megan is."

Layla's voice, when she answered, was taut. "This is not a good time."

"What's going on? Is Megan with you?"

"He's calling *you*?" He heard Megan speak in the background.

"Tell me what's going on? She sounds upset. Put her on."

"Believe me, you don't want that. We're on our way back right now," Layla said and hung up.

What the hell?

"Something is up, Megan sounded *pissed off* in the background but I don't know why."

Adam laughed. "Well, let's hazard a guess, shall we? You called her sister instead of her. Her sister who you have seen naked and had sex with. This has to be uncomfortable for her."

"I didn't know her number. I didn't even know *her* before this afternoon! How can I have called her? And I didn't know when I served as Layla's Anchor I'd be mated to her sister. I'm barely even a damned werewolf. I didn't ask for any of this."

"Well, I'm sorry you got stuck with me. And I'm really sorry you seem to be so horrified by what you are. By what I am."

He closed his eyes at the sound of Megan's voice. At the hurt there. He turned around to face her and felt some hurt of his own when he reached toward her and she stepped back.

"I don't feel like I'm stuck with you. I was just frustrated. I heard you in the background, I knew you were upset. I hated not knowing why." He was constrained by everyone looking on, damn it.

Adam stepped smoothly into the fray by hugging

Megan. When he stepped back he cupped her face in
his hands. "Congratulations, honey. I know this is hard
and it was totally unexpected but it's a gift. Don't forget that, okay? Why don't we all get something to eat?
Calm down. You only heard part of the conversation.
The rest was me being honored to be asked to be your
Anchor. That is, if you'll have me?"

"I can't deal with this," Megan said so quietly Shane
had to strain to hear it. The pain in her voice, the confusion was clear though.

Adam put his arms around her and swayed a bit from
side to side. "Why don't the three of us go somewhere?
Hmm? Where it's quiet and we can talk this all through.
It's been a big day and you're both caught off guard.
Come on, honey. You're upset and there are a lot of
people out here."

Layla watched Shane through wary eyes and he hated
it. He hated that he couldn't just talk this over with her
without making everyone else upset.

Megan looked up and he only wanted her, wanted to
make things right for her, for the two of them.

"What do you say? We can meet up with your family later on. Will you accept Adam as your Anchor?"
He moved to her, brushing the hair from her forehead
and he felt her anguish unknot at the simple gesture.
What a strange and comforting thing the bond was. He
knew, had heard, that the bond was intense but words
couldn't do it justice. Part of him wondered how in the
world his mother could feel this for his father and yet
not love all of him. He wondered if his father resented it.

"Let's all go to my room. I'll need to stick close to
Nina but I'm sure she can keep her mitts off the door
and leave us alone. We can talk there."

She took the hand he held out and Adam sent him a smile and moved to her other side. Layla and her sisters kept a watchful eye on them as they moved back inside the hotel.

Chapter Four

She stepped aside and motioned them both into the room. It wasn't a suite or anything so there wasn't much space to sit or hang out other than the bed. It seemed oddly intimate but Megan supposed they were far beyond that if she was going to actually have sex with Adam too.

Not like she had much to complain over, Adam shared the Rosario genes and was just as handsome as Sid and Shane were. And she knew him. Knew him better than she knew Shane, which was comforting and disconcerting all at once.

"Shane, you understand that Adam is part of my extended family right? We'll see him all the time." She tossed her things off the bed and patted it. They joined her, Shane making sure his leg touched hers.

"Like you'll have to get used to my bond with Layla?"

"I have no other choice, do I? And you're awfully flip. We'll see how you feel after this." She shrugged. "You don't live nearby. You don't have a typical anchor relationship. In fact, with the way an anchor bond usually works, the Anchor needs to be as powerful or more than the mated pair and/or related to the male. I'm really only convinced this will work because you've lived outside a Pack so you don't really have any hierarchal relationship and Adam is your cousin. But you know, it's harder when the bond is new and the Anchor isn't mated yet. I just want to talk about this up front. We rushed into the bond and I want this to work."

"You're assuming we'll live in Seattle? I have a life in Las Vegas."

She nodded. "I know you do. And I know your job is important to you, I respect that. I honor it because it's important to you. But I'm going to tell you up front, I won't live Packless. I'm a werewolf and I am not ashamed of it. I want to live around other wolves. It's who we are, Shane."

"We should talk about this after the tri-bond when Adam is gone."

She chewed her lip and looked to Adam who shrugged. "I'll take care of you, you know that. If Shane stays in Vegas, I'll be there for you every day. We only live five miles apart. You two can visit back and forth. You need the Anchor, Megan. You already claimed her, Shane, it's too late to try and negotiate on this. You aren't dating, you're mated. You claimed her and you may not live as a wolf but you sure as hell know what you did and you did it anyway. You know there could have been others for her if you hadn't claimed her. Eventually she'd have found another mate out there. You took that step knowing you can't take it back. Suck it up and deal."

"If you like, you can leave while we do the tri-bond. I'll call you when it's over or we can meet downstairs or whatever." The warmth that'd crept back into her eyes ebbed away when she looked to him again. He didn't like it one bit. He may not know what the hell they'd do about their living situation but he knew they'd be together somehow. His parents made it work somehow, didn't they?

As for the tri-bond, there was no fucking way on Earth he was going to let her have sex with Adam without him there. He didn't mean to hurt her, didn't want to. They had to work this out and it wasn't going to happen if he let her distance herself.

He moved to her and she lay back on the bed, looking up into his face. Her hair tumbled around her head, her lips slightly parted.

She reached up, touching his face and he turned into her palm, pressing a kiss there. She smiled and he did too. Megan Warden was truly beautiful.

Adam stayed where he'd been sitting, waiting for them to make a decision and Shane turned back to his cousin after brushing his lips over Megan's just to steal a taste.

"I want to be here when you seal the tri-bond."

Adam nodded. "All right. Is this okay with you, Megan? Do you trust me?"

She sat up and took Adam's hand, kissing it. "I do. I'm honored you'd do this for us."

Adam laughed and then looked to Shane, who joined him. "Megan, do you think it's a punishment to serve as your Anchor? To touch you that way? You're—" he shrugged "—incredibly desirable. Smart. Strong. I'm the lucky one. It's me who's honored."

"And you're okay with seeing me with another male?" Megan turned back to Shane.

He thought it over carefully. The anchor bond was something he accepted. Clearly it was a safety issue for her and God knew he wanted her protected. He remembered how on edge Layla had been when he'd stepped in as her Anchor because she'd gone several days after the claiming without an Anchor. At the same time, it did it for him that another man found her sexy.

Not a very typical fetish, he supposed, but common enough. He liked to watch and he knew no one would ever be to her what he was so it took away any real fear of losing her to anyone else. All the thrill, none of the negatives.

"Yes," he said, knowing from the way her eyes were lit that she'd picked up just how aroused he was.

A smile bloomed over her lips, bursting into his gut. He watched hungrily as she lay back down. Slowly, she trailed fingertips up her thighs, her skirt sliding upward, and then over her mound and breasts. After that, she stretched her arms up above her head and left them there.

"Then I suppose someone should help me out of these sandals."

The breath rushed from Adam's lips and Shane knew exactly what he meant.

"You get the sandals, I'll get the shirt and bra and meet you in the middle." Shane sent her a wicked grin and she laughed.

"I'm all yours. But I'd like to put in a request for you two to be naked as well. We rushed before, I haven't been able to see much."

Adam whipped his shirt away and got off the bed. Megan's heart thudded in her chest to be the center of these two males' attention. Both of them so sexy and clearly attracted to her. She'd never had a threesome with two men before so she sure as hell planned to make the most of it.

Shane took her chin in his fingers and turned her to face him. Which she happily did as he got rid of his shirt and then slowly unbuttoned and unzipped his jeans and stepped from them.

"Whoo," she whispered. His boxer briefs slid down impressively hard thighs and he stood there totally naked and obviously not that disappointed about a three-some because his cock was so hard it tapped his belly. "Dr. Rosario, you do keep in shape."

She looked over to Adam who'd finished undressing and leaned over her feet to get her sandals off.

Where Shane was big and broad, Adam was shorter although no less broad. She didn't know too many long and lean wolves like Sid. Adam's longer hair slid forward, obscuring his face. But the part that wasn't obscured was also quite pleased to be part of this scenario. Gentle fingers untied the straps and removed her shoes, kneading her feet once he was done.

Megan groaned and stretched, enjoying the feeling for long moments.

He looked up at her groan and smiled. "I'd like to kiss you." Adam looked to Shane to make sure everyone was in and Shane nodded.

"I'd like that too." She got to her knees and leaned toward his lips and he met her halfway. Dimly she realized Shane had pulled her shirt and bra off, the clever man.

Shane's hands caressed her back and shoulders as Adam's mouth met hers. It was just a hint of a kiss, an appetizer. He drew back and she realized they were all wading in so carefully.

Truth be told, what she felt for Shane, she knew would be forever. It was what the mate bond was. She needed him, yes. She wanted him, lusted after him, wanted to know him. But she didn't love him. She might have felt more intensely for him if he'd been more enthusiastic about the bond but at that moment she knew they could work toward love and with work, they'd achieve it. But right then she was just as turned on by Adam as she was by Shane, although for different reasons.

There was no doubt in Megan's mind that she'd never cheat on Shane or step outside their bond. She wouldn't, period. Didn't want to. It wasn't who she was and it wasn't what she envisioned for herself and her mate. After this day, it would be just her and Shane unless they agreed otherwise and she doubted that would happen, at least not for a long time after they'd established their relationship and their trust level with each other.

She turned to Shane and sifted her fingers through his dark hair, his eyes closed halfway and he pressed into her touch.

"I want you to enjoy this. I like to watch, Megan. I like that he'll have you this once, have what's mine because I allow it. But never again." He whispered it like a confession, like an offering of something intimate and she took it as such.

It meant something, more than just something physical.

A hint of a smile played at the corner of his mouth just before it met hers. All amusement dissolved as the passion in his kiss sizzled against her. He traced the curve of her lips with his tongue. As if he was memorizing their shape. His teeth grazed her bottom lip as he sucked it into his mouth. Electric heat arced down her spine, bringing her body into an arch.

His taste wended through her, marking her, spoiling her for any other as she sucked at his tongue. She felt the mattress dip behind her as Adam settled in at her back, pulling her skirt and panties down. Shane pulled away, having her lean on him as Adam finished undressing her. Desire-stunned, she angled herself so she could see them both, totally naked.

Her eyes widened at the sheer beauty of those two masculine bodies. Holy shit, Shane was gorgeous. He was what could only be described accurately as "ripped." Not just a muscled stomach but an honest to fucking goodness six-pack. The muscles ran tight over his ribs, across his shoulders and down his chest. He was absolutely stunning. When he caught the appraisal and appreciation in her gaze, a sexy smile broke over his face.

"I love how you look at me."

She laughed. "I can't not look at you." She moved her gaze to Adam and his tawny skin. Shane's looks were big and masculine but also had an elegance to them. But Adam was more feral, brawny, just barely leashed. His hair was longer, his eyes were wilder. "And you aren't a chore to stare at either." She shrugged with a laugh. "Well, let's get started, shall we?"

Ensorcelled by the sight of Shane, the heat of his skin, she leaned toward him, bending her head. The scent of his soap and the musk of his cologne ribboned through her. She scented herself on him still from earlier and it tightened things low. She flicked her tongue over his nipple, first one and then the other, liking the way he groaned in response.

He arched his hips forward, clearly wanting her touch, her tongue, elsewhere. Reaching out, she ran the tips of her fingers up the length of his cock. The silk of his skin, hot and hard, greeted her senses. The musk of his scent reached her and she had to close her eyes a moment against the feral appeal.

Swallowing against the raw need that rode her, she grinned at him. "My, my, my. So much to touch and taste."

Adam moved behind her, kissing across her shoulders and, not wanting to ignore him, she turned around to face him. He pulled her against his naked chest so they were skin to skin. When her mouth opened on a gasp of pleasure at the sensation, he lowered his lips to hers, kissing her hard. His hands, large and strong, ran down the small of her back, over the curve of her ass and thighs. Needing to get to the heart of the matter, her hands went for his cock and he hissed his pleasure at her touch.

Shane laughed, pressing himself against her back, his cock pressing into the soft flesh of her ass. "You're so fucking sexy here wedged between us. I've never seen anything so damned sexy in my life." He left a warm, wet trail as he dragged his tongue from her ear down her neck and shoulder, holding her head arched back using her hair.

Her nipples met the hard muscle of Adam's chest and he moved from side to side, grazing them with his own. Megan arched her back, tipping her head back so Shane could continue to kiss her neck.

"Ready for step two?" Moist heat spread from her ear down her body.

"Hmm?" she managed as she ran her nails down Adam's ribs.

"We're moving to the fucking portion of the day's

events. Just making sure you're still with us," Shane murmured in her ear, nibbling the lobe, leaving goose bumps in his wake.

She laughed at that but it strangled into a moan as Adam's mouth slid down the upper curve of her right breast and his tongue circled her nipple. "Are you kidding? This is like the women's version of a 'Penthouse Letter.'"

"Well then, let's get to it." Shane bit the tendon where neck met shoulder and she nearly lost her mind.

Adam took a nipple between his teeth, sending shivers of delight up and down her torso. She had one hand buried in his hair and reached back with the other to hold Shane to her. Shane smoothed his hands down her body, moved around to her belly and parted her pussy with one hand, slowly making the circuit from her gate back up around her clit and back again with clever fingers.

The three of them moved as one unit, writhing, making soft sounds of arousal. Megan tugged on Shane's hair to bring his mouth closer as she craned her neck to kiss him. Her hips churned restlessly, jerking forward as he pinched her clit every few circuits. Bright shards of pleasure burst through her, heating her, driving her upward. Adam moved to the other breast to console that ignored nipple.

Just the smell of male skin and arousal, the feel of those hard bodies writhing against hers sent Megan hurtling over the edge into a teeth-grindingly intense orgasm.

"Oh yes, like that, ohgod ohgod ohgod," she whispered into Shane's mouth as her body trembled.

Finally Adam pulled back and Shane moved his

hand. The cocky smile on Adam's face had faded into a look of intense concentration. "On your belly."

She shivered as Shane put a pillow beneath her hips to prop her up. She so loved being fucked this way. A gentle but firm hand arranged her just-so, leaving her wide-open to him, ass in the air, thighs spread wide. The broad head of Adam's cock brushed against the slick-hot gate to her pussy and he pushed in slowly.

She sucked in her breath sharply. Her eyes rolled up into her head at the pleasure of the thickness of him filling her up, stroking those nerve endings deep inside her. More, she wanted more. She rolled her hips to push back against him, meeting his thrust.

With a soft grunt, he pressed in totally to the root, the short, wiry hair at the base of his cock tickling against the bare lips of her pussy. He ran his hands along her back and around to her breasts.

"No," Shane said, swatting Adam's hands. "Those are mine." She had to make the effort to open her eyes but it was worth it to catch the sight of his wicked grin as he scooted in front of her.

"That'll make it hard for me to put that gorgeous cock in my mouth then won't it?" Megan asked as her voice went slurred a bit when Adam began to draw out of her.

Shane's eyes lit with approval. "You're quite right."

Adam's hands went back to her breasts, rolling the nipples between his fingers, shooting fire right to her clit. She thrust back against him and looked Shane in the eyes, running her tongue around her lips in invitation. Their connection tautened, strengthened and relief slid though her.

He scooted toward her and, without preamble, she

lowered her mouth down around his cock and he shuddered on a moan. The rhythm of Adam's slow and tortuous in and out and her slow and tortuous up and down was incredibly intense. It seemed like rather than three people, they were one machine, moving on each other, the flow of pleasure heightened with each pass. Still, despite the pleasure of having two men in her at once, it was Shane she felt inside her. In her heart, in her brain, in her bones.

Adam's pace began to get restless, he started to speed up and add force, his nice fat cock battering into her as she arched up to meet him. Shane was close, his balls drawn up into his body, his cock rock hard, his breathing shallow. Megan knew he watched not just her mouth on his cock but Adam fucking into her body.

"I'm almost there, Megan. Come with me." Adam gritted out. She grabbed one of his hands and guided it to her swollen clit. He took the hint and ran his thumb over it, mashing it as his thrusts became more frenzied.

Shane's hands fisted in her hair as he thrust upward into her mouth. She worked to stay relaxed even as orgasm began to make itself known in her body once again. Just as she knew it would hit, Shane's came first. He moaned long and low, his cock pulsing time and again and she worked to hold climax for herself back until he was done, wanting to draw every bit of his pleasure into herself first.

Finally as he softened in her mouth, she gave his cock one last parting kiss and pulled up, opening herself to her orgasm. It came, hard and fast, painting stars against her closed eyelids as Adam grunted out his own, slamming against her, grabbing her hips so hard she knew there would be bruises. Moments later they collapsed into a heap onto Shane's legs, the three of them spent, working to catch their breath for several minutes as the anchor bond settled into place, making her whole, bringing Adam into their lives forever.

At long last Adam pulled out and helped Megan settle on her side. He got out of bed and kissed her temple. "I'm going to go for now. That was amazing. I'm always going to be here for you if you need me. You two just be together. I'll see you in a bit."

Megan opened her eyes, and smiled as she watched him get dressed and head to the door.

"Thank you, Adam. For everything." She waved.

He laughed. "It was my pleasure. Thank *you*. Thank you both."

And he was gone.

Shane didn't speak for a long while. What had just happened was intense and wonderful on many levels and he didn't want to spoil it with words. He brought her against his body, spooning her to himself, content to breathe her in as they got their breath back.

"Wow," Shane finally said softly. "I can't, there aren't words for how beautiful you were, how hot it was to see you between us that way. You're amazing." He nuzzled her neck and she sighed, wriggling back into him. His cock stirred, happily ready to take her again. He did have to admit that was one of the best things about being a werewolf.

"It was awesome. And it feels like you're ready to go again."

"Can you take me?"

She turned in his arms, big green eyes looking up

into his face, seeing right to the very heart of him. "I want you inside me."

He hugged her then, before rolling off the bed to stand. Reaching out, he dragged her to the edge of the mattress. Slowly, seductively, Megan stretched one leg up and around his body, spreading herself open for him. The bed was the perfect height for this.

She was so fucking beautiful there spread out just for him like a banquet. He tested her, finding her wet and swollen from their last round. Her clit was slippery and sensitive and she caught her breath as he flicked his fingertips over it.

She wrapped her legs around him and pulled him closer, grabbing his cock and guiding him true. When the head of his cock entered her, he stilled.

Her eyes, those beautiful eyes looked up into his and he felt something deep inside him stir and unfurl. With the late afternoon sun glinting off her pale skin, she glowed like alabaster. Tri-bond established at last, she was all his. Forever.

He felt a pulse of her honey scald his balls. Smiling down at her, he hilted with one last press into her, loving the way her pussy fluttered and clutched his cock.

She sighed and stretched, arching her back toward him. "So very nice," she murmured lazily.

"Mmm. I'm in total agreement." He dragged himself out of her tight, slick heat and thrust back in. What a fucking understatement that was.

"Yes," he said, unable to speak again for a few moments, "I'm going to need to do this every fucking day."

The pace was slow, leisurely but intense. Their gazes locked together, they didn't need to speak much because their bodies said everything needed saying. All uncertainty of where he'd live and what their next steps would be didn't matter compared to what they were with each other right then. What they would always be.

The depth of that connection shook him. He wanted to fall to his knees and thank the heavens for it, for the way it made him feel totally right and whole. But also to rail and cry because he truly felt the depth of his disassociation with who and what he was in his togetherness with Megan. The contrast of the two halves of his existence shook him deeply.

There was only her, he had to stop thinking about anything but her. They didn't say anything further as he quickened his thrusts. That is, until she began to beg. If she only knew, if he only could reveal that dark place deep within him, the part that loved to make a woman beg.

"Please, please, please," she whispered over and over.

"Please?" A slow grin broke over his face.

"Oh God yes, please," Megan answered, nodding, sending all that gold hair into disarray.

"Hmm, maybe I'll just, you know, get a sandwich and come back in a few minutes." He grinned at her. Until she shifted so she could reach around and cup his balls, running her fingernails over them, palming them at the same time. She undulated her hips, her inner muscles squeezing and stroking his cock until beads of sweat popped out on his forehead. Her satisfied smile made him laugh.

"Okay so the sandwich can wait. Yes. Oh yeah, like that." He bit out the words as he began to fuck her hard and fast. The sound of skin slapping skin reverberated through the room as he watched her breasts moving up and down as he thrust. He wanted to crawl inside her and stay there for the duration.

She arched and he adjusted his entry so that on each thrust the length of his cock brushed against her clit. Those desire-heavy, half-lidded eyes flew open as she gasped. Her cunt spasmed around his cock as she came.

A ragged moan came from him as the echoes of her orgasm through her pussy dragged him into his own climax. He thrust harder then, his back straightened and, deep within her, his cock unloaded as he growled low and yet loud.

Finally, he collapsed onto her, both their bodies still partly off the bed, her legs still clasped around his waist. Chest to chest, their hearts pounded, rebounding off the other as the sweat cooled and breathing normalized.

He looked at the digital clock next to the bed and realized his entire universe had changed in less than six hours.

Chapter Five

By the time they got back downstairs, it was already dark and people were ready to go to dinner.

"Gorgeous, I just heard the news!"

Megan heard the voice and smiled as she turned into arms already surrounding her in a hug. "When did you get here?"

Josh, the Pacific Pack's Enforcer gave her a full kiss on the lips and Shane growled, yanking him back.

"Whoa!" Megan and Tracy both stepped in. "He's Tracy's Enforcer and he's just congratulating me. It's all right. He's a wolf, he knows I'm mated."

"He's putting his hands on my mate, that's not all right."

God help her, Megan found herself totally charmed by that bit of silly possessiveness.

"I'm sorry," Josh said, holding his hands up, palms out. "I've known Megan a few years and she's like my baby sister. I should have realized you'd be offended. I'm Josh, can we start over?"

Shane relaxed but kept his arm around Megan. "Apology accepted. I'm Shane."

They shook hands and Layla laughed in the background along with Nina.

"Not that I'm not pleased to see you but what are you doing here?" Megan asked Josh.

"I called him down. Or rather, after I spoke to Nick and Gabe about you mating, we thought it would be good to have another Enforcer here so you two could have some time alone." Tracy took Megan's hand. "You can take a vacation and just be with Shane without worrying about Nina or Cascadia for at least a week."

Nina moved to her. "Hiro is here too. Lex and I spoke earlier, Hiro will take over your spot as my guard here and back home. Lex wants you to take some time. He said for you to call him when you wanted to talk."

She smiled. Her brother, all tough, still a big marshmallow inside when it came to the people he loved.

"That's a good idea, Megan." Shane kissed her neck where he'd bitten her. He may not want to admit he was a wolf, but he sure fucked like one. "We can go to my place for a week or so. I can take the time off. We can get to know each other."

She agreed. They needed time away from Layla and Cascadia and all their various responsibilities. There was so much to work out. She wasn't overly thrilled by going to Vegas, which was his turf, but at the same time, he'd be giving up a lot if she could convince him to move to Seattle so it was only fair she go.

"Why don't you and Lay have a drink or go to dinner to catch up? I'll just say goodbye and eat with my family and then we can leave?" She turned to him, loving the way he pulled her close.

"Are you sure? You'll be all right with it? You know you have nothing to worry about." He kissed her and then again.

She smiled. "I do. My sister and I worked it out. I

have to trust you and our bond. And Adam will be at dinner with us so…" She shrugged. "It'll take some getting used to but we're adults."

He grinned. "I'll meet you back here in an hour. One hour. Then we'll go. I'll get us some airline tickets."

She tiptoed up and kissed him, liking the way his whiskers felt against her lips. "Okay."

Shane noted Layla whispering to Megan and hugging her before she nodded and headed toward him. He had to admit seeing Megan take Adam's hand on one side and her mother's on the other was slightly disconcerting.

"Don't sweat the tickets. Cade pulled some super Alpha mojo and there'll be a private plane waiting for you two at John Wayne. Let's go grab something to eat. There's a little café just near the adults-only pool." Layla took his arm and they walked the other way, but not until after he'd caught Megan laughing at something someone said and his stomach twisted at how beautiful she was.

"So," Layla said as they sat down, "you're going to have to face who you are now. Once and for all." She looked up at the server who'd approached. "Can I get an iced tea and a turkey sandwich with fries?"

"Give me a cheeseburger, fries and a soda, please."

The server nodded and disappeared.

"What do you mean?" Although he knew exactly what she meant.

She sighed. "Okay let's pretend for a few. First of all, congratulations. Really. I couldn't have wished a better mate for you than Megan. She's going to be good for you. Speaking of family, Sid says to tell you hello and the kids loved the DVD player. I told you not to send one, by the way. No one listens to me. They're spoiled enough."

"I just saw his mother two weeks ago when they came through Vegas. And the kids needed a DVD player. I'm a doctor, I have a few extra pennies."

She rolled her eyes. "So you say every time you send them presents. You really should let me tell people how good you are with the kids. I don't know why you insist on pretending you aren't that involved in our life."

"It's about expectations, you know that. If people knew I saw them and had more contact with them than they thought, I'd suddenly be expected to go to all this werewolf junk. And you know how I feel about that. I want to be left alone to do my own thing. It hasn't hurt my father to live without it all these years. You guys are like a cult or something."

She flipped him off. "A cult? You mean like, oh, say, a family who cares about you and stuff? Oooh, scary! Is that what your mother tells you, Shane? That what you are is a cult? Is that why every time I see your father, Sid and I and the kids hug up on him as much as possible because he misses contact with his own kind so desperately? Is that how you want to be? I know she's your mother, I'm not trying to hurt you but, Shane, she's harmed you in a big way. You're a werewolf. Not a human. We're different. Not wrong, not bad, just different. The human women you date can't fill that part of you. And they really can't now." She laughed. "Because well, that part would be ripped off and bloody if Megan caught you."

"Ha, ha." He winced. "I'm no cheater, thank you very much. Anyway, I've heard the werewolf pitch, I'm not interested in hearing it again."

"Too damned bad. The whole *werewolf thing*, Shane, is that you've been raised to hate yourself but deep down inside you know it's not right. When you allow yourself to feel what you're *supposed* to feel, you understand that. Let go and be who you are." She paused. "Megan is a really grounded woman. Probably the most grounded person I've ever known. She's dedicated to her job. She's good to her family. She's the kind of person who takes the garbage out for the elderly woman who lives across the street from her on garbage day. Megan believes in community. You have been raised to be suspicious of half your identity and I'm not going to get into it any more at this point." She held up a hand as he automatically began to defend his mother. "The issue is, Megan is a werewolf. She's a Warden. You may not get this because you haven't known her very long but she's a powerful werewolf and she won't leave what she is behind to be a human doctor's wife in the suburbs outside Las Vegas. It would kill her."

The food arrived and he shoved it down automatically, knowing he needed the calories but also wanting to avoid speaking as he gathered his thoughts.

"I have a life. I don't know why everyone assumes I should be the one to give it all up for her because she has a job. Well, I have a job too. I've got a nice practice in Vegas. Friends."

"Friends? A life? I'm going to tell you this because I love you and you're someone special to me. You have a nice house and you have human women you fuck. You have people you go to nightclubs with but they don't know you. You don't share your life with them above that. Those aren't friends and that's not a life. And she doesn't have a *job*, Shane. She's got a calling. What she is isn't something she can just re-license somewhere else. You're asking her to be what you are. To pretend to be something she's not. She is Pack. She's a wolf. She needs to be around other wolves."

"I love you too, Lay, but this isn't your business." He shrugged hoping he looked nonchalant. "This is between me and Megan. I'm not some beta wolf who'll come running when she snaps her fingers."

Layla looked up at him, anger sparking in her gaze. "Don't. Don't even try it. Not with me, buster. In the first place, don't you minimize what Megan is to you. In the second place, don't minimize what you've done. *You've* done. You sealed the bond. You did it knowing what would happen. Suck. It. Up. Be a damned grown up, do you hear me? Do not mess with my sister's head. If you think I'm being harsh you had better prepare yourself. You screwed yourself right into the mother-lode of Pack law. Megan has risked her life multiple times for the wolves who lead your people. *Your people*, Shane. You are a werewolf." She wiped her mouth and stood. "You can pay with your pennies. I'm going to go help get Megan packed. If I know her, she skipped dinner and is up in her room giving Hiro orders on how to protect Nina. Don't be a dumbass. I love you. She'll come to love you. You have to love yourself and believe that what you are, what you were born, is not something wrong or bad."

She bent to kiss his cheek and stalked away.

Megan had waved goodbye to her family and climbed up the stairs to the private plane Cade had waiting for them at the airport. The flight to Las Vegas was a quick one and like a tourist, she watched out the window as they circled to land, mouth agape at the gorgeous lights on the Strip.

On the way to his house, Megan sat, nestled into Shane's side as he drove his sporty little car. He'd not stopped touching her since he'd shown up at her room door, a to-go bag in his hand and a smile on his face. She'd wondered why Layla had shown up early but she was happy to spend time with her sister before they left.

He didn't live too far away from town and the air was reasonably clean albeit still very warm even at midnight. She had known him twelve hours and her life was totally different than where it had been when she'd tumbled out of bed that morning hoping to buy shoes and shoot guns.

"A gated community, huh?" she murmured as the large iron gates swung open silently. A guard tipped his hat as they drove past.

"It's a nice, safe place to live. You'll like it here."

Nice wasn't really how she'd have described his house. *Palatial* would be more accurate. He pulled into the garage where a motorcycle sat and a boat was parked, covered up.

"We're home. Come on, let me show you around."

"Lex has a Harley too. You two can go riding. Nina hates it and Dave lives in Boston now so he doesn't have as many friends to ride with."

He smiled absently as he keyed in a code and opened the door leading into the house. The place was huge inside. Marble and gleaming hardwoods and tiles. Abstract art hanging on the walls. No pictures of people or wolves. No books. Several plasma screens in the rooms she passed. No throws on the backs of the couches.

"Do you like it?" He flipped on the lights and she

saw through the glass he had a pool. Those lights went on as well. It was beautiful in its own way.

"It's beautiful." She nodded. Nothing she'd ever want and it didn't seem to really express much about him either. But what did she know? She'd known him half a day.

"You're probably tired. Let's get your suitcase up to the bedroom. Well, to our bedroom. Do you want some tea? Are you hungry?"

He led her up an open staircase and into his room. She couldn't really feel like it was hers. The room was stark white with a big bed in the center. Everything in the room was white. Just not something she'd have chosen. But she made herself stop reacting to it and just try and get to know him.

"I need a shower I think."

He put her suitcase down and pushed open double doors to her left. "Bathroom's right there. Towels are in the cabinet. I'm going to check my messages and make some arrangements to have extra time off. I'll be back up in a bit." He kissed her and left her to her own devices as he headed out.

Somewhere in the back of her senses, another woman's scent lived. She'd been here, that other woman, but not for a while. There were no female touches in the bathroom and as she pulled her toiletries out, she noted with some satisfaction that not a single tampon or other female emergency product was in evidence in the drawers. Not that she peeked. Much.

The bathroom was so neat, so tidy she felt odd even taking her clothes off. Boy were they opposites. It would take some work to feel comfortable with each other she knew. She guessed it would be good to start by folding up her discarded clothes and putting them neatly on the counter instead of tossing them to the side like she would at home.

It was well after midnight but he left voice mails with his staff and service and got another doctor to cover his patients for an extra two days, giving them until Wednesday before he had to deal with the reality of work again.

Cynthia would be awake still, despite the late hour, her shift would only have ended about an hour before. He heard the water begin to run and dialed her cell.

"I wasn't expecting to hear from you," she answered without preamble. "Bored in LA already?"

Cynthia, the woman he'd been seeing for the past several months. Mostly exclusively but not in a serious way, only that he just didn't have much time to pursue anyone else. She was young, twenty-four, and worked as a cocktail waitress at a casino.

"I'm home actually."

"Oh is this a booty call?" She laughed.

"Ahh, no. Cynthia, I'm just calling to let you know I met someone." He hadn't been with her in over a week due to his work schedule. But he didn't want to take a risk and have her show up and be a nasty surprise for Megan. He didn't want to be an ass and lead Cynthia on either.

"That was unexpected. But okay. Do I know her?"

"No. She's not from Vegas. Anyway, I just wanted to let you know. You're a nice woman and I didn't want you to think I was double-dealing or anything."

"Good luck and give me a call if things don't work out."

He hung up. That was easier than he thought it'd be but he was relieved as hell. He'd have to tell Megan at some point just so there'd be nothing between them she didn't know.

Smiling, he headed back upstairs. His woman probably needed some help scrubbing her back.

Chapter Six

The next morning he woke slowly, rising to consciousness but aware Megan lay within his arms. Her hair spread over his arm and shoulder, the scent of her sliding into his system with each breath he took.

She was warm and loose, one breast pressed against his naked torso, one arm over his chest, her skin pale over his more olive tones. He simply took her in, watching the rise and fall of her body.

Before too long, her nipple, the one pressed to his body, tightened and he scented the heated response of her desire. She had awakened wanting him as much as he wanted her, apparently.

"Morning," he murmured. He brought her hand to his mouth for a kiss and that one brief touch of his tongue against the skin of her knuckle sent need sizzling through him.

"Mmm," she hummed and stretched, turning into his body, sliding a silky thigh up his and over his aching cock.

Writhing, warm and willing woman and all his. Suddenly he was awake, wide-awake and ready to take every bit she wanted to give him and then coax some more. He rolled over so she was on her back beneath him and he nearly cried out for joy when she spread her legs and made room for him. Like he was made to be there.

"Fuck me," she said in a low voice. Velvet and seductive much like every damned inch of her skin.

"Let me build up to it." Even as he said it, he couldn't stop himself from dragging the head of his cock through her pussy, the heat of her making him crazy.

"I don't want that. I want you in me. You can be finessed while we shower. For now, I want you and I don't want you to hold back. I want everything from you."

His heart stuttered even as he angled himself, hitched her thigh up over his hip and thrust into her pussy.

Over and over he filled her and retreated, her body welcoming him, her gaze locked with his, those sleepy, sexy green eyes seeing right to the heart of him. Connected this way, through their intense sexual chemistry, he felt truly himself with her.

He didn't know if he could give her everything of himself. But he could share this way. He could love her with every part of his body and show her the gift he thought she was. Clearly they had a great sexual connection, maybe that would get them through, take them to another level. But right then, all he wanted to do was drown in her body, revel in her beauty and empty himself deep inside her before they stumbled into the shower and he showed her the novelty of just exactly how all those extra shower heads could aid him when he was on his knees, licking her clit until she screamed his name.

This could be enough. For now it could be enough.

He watched as she pulled her hair back into a sleek ponytail and laughed with the guy behind the counter.

He'd never actually been to a shooting range before so it was an entirely new experience when she'd told him that morning they were off to American Shooter Supply just a few miles off the Strip.

All the men behind the counter were as enamored of her as Shane was. She moved easily in her skin, her hands graceful and yet very sure as she signed the forms and took her driver's license back.

"You sure you don't want to shoot with me?" She turned to him, holding a plastic container with a black matte handgun inside. She'd surprised him when she'd pulled that out of her suitcase.

"Um, not this time. I'll just watch." He indicated the tables set up in front of the clear glass separating the shooting area from the counter space.

She shrugged and went through the first set of doors, put on sound-deadening headphones and then through the second set. Confidently she moved to the space directly in front of where he sat and placed her things down.

Was he wrong to find the eye protection she wore hot? They weren't just utilitarian but had a streamlined, sexy style to them. No one else looked so good. Her ass looked really tasty, high and tight in the jeans she wore. Her legs just went on and on as she moved to stand with her feet braced, slightly apart. And then the muscles in her upper arms bunched when she aimed and began to fire.

She was beautiful in her strength. In her agility and the way she wore her violence so casually. Not as a threat. He didn't see that she scared anyone, or that she used her ability and feral nature to bully. But it was clearly part of her in a way she considered just as normal as the color of her hair or the set of her eyes.

Every moment he spent with her, every new thing they did other than sex—although the sex was amazing—drew him into her more. Two days after they'd arrived in Las Vegas and had bonded, he found himself really liking Megan. Not just as a woman he was chemically bonded to, but as the person he could begin to see spending his life with.

She had this way of scrunching up her face when she was describing something to him that made him want to kiss her. He found himself waking up early to watch her work out. He wasn't even annoyed with the way she tossed her stuff around the house, filling everything with her presence.

Which scared him. Even as he was mesmerized by the way she calmly shot the target in the heart and in between the eyes over and over with deadly accuracy, he felt as though he was drowning in her.

He didn't know if it was her, the bond, how he really felt or what. He felt it, that was true, but the human part of him approached the bond warily. Yes, he'd claimed her without a second thought. Believed in the bond as he sat there and watched this woman who'd weaved herself into his world in so short a time. At the same time, resentment lingered. Was it real? This other person was suddenly everything to him in a way he'd never experienced, not even with Layla.

It was as if his wolf had surfaced and wouldn't cede any space to the human part of him when it came to this woman, when it came to this part of his life. Never had any woman, anyone for that matter, been so all important to him.

* * *

The sharp scent of cordite had kept Megan centered on the task. Squeeze. Bam. Squeeze. Bam. Over and over. Each physical action on her part created a bigger hole in the target. She liked it. The result before her eyes. She could control it, knowing the outcome each time because she'd practiced over and over until she mastered it.

It wasn't the same with him. She didn't try to control her world with hyperorganized living space like he did. But they were both control freaks just the same. Shane was someone who set her totally off balance and she did not like to be unsure and uneasy. She had a life where things mattered. Where what she did made a difference. That was her control. Here she felt as if she were spinning her wheels, just waiting for him to make a decision. Tension hung in the air between them. Expectancy, hesitation. It was ridiculous. She knew something had to move, be dealt with. *Something.* How long she'd wait wasn't a decision she'd come to yet.

The next day, as they ate lunch on the terrace of a fashionable restaurant in an area of the city away from the Strip, she felt his hesitation like a physical thing between them.

He didn't hold back in bed. He loved every inch of her body with no reservation at all. But away from bed it was a different story. Despite his telling her she should feel at home in the house, it was his house still. He didn't want to speak of the future, only asking that they take it day by day.

At first, it was something she did albeit with reservations but now it felt different. She felt uncomfortable with him at times in a way she hadn't felt with anyone in her life. This was her mate! Another wolf who was meant to make her feel whole and cherished and instead, a sense of anxiety set in and hadn't left.

As they sat, pretending nothing was wrong, a group of people approached the table. "Shane! How are you?"

A tall bottle-blonde leaned down and kissed him square on the mouth.

Calmly, Megan took the woman's arm and yanked her back. "He's fine but his mouth is off-limits to you for anything but speaking."

Shane laughed but discomfort threaded the sound. It was all so fake, his world and Megan hated it.

"This is Cynthia, an old friend. Cynthia, this is Megan, the woman I told you about."

The blonde looked Megan over. Megan knew what *friend* meant in that context but it didn't matter then. What she found interesting was his comment about him telling Cynthia about her. When had that happened?

"Oh, well then. Shane you know everyone." She indicated the people with her with a lazy wave. Cynthia didn't bother introducing them to Megan and apparently it wasn't important to Shane either.

There was some talking about things Megan wasn't clued in on. She didn't get the feeling he was ashamed or being rude but that he didn't know how to bring her into his world.

Her phone rang. "I'm sorry, I need to take this." She stood up and moved into a far corner, not wanting to disturb anyone's meal to take Lex's call. They might not have manners but she did.

"I'm just checking in on you. How are things?"

She smiled at the sound of her brother's voice. "It's

warm. Sunny. I'm eating some pretty something on a pretty plate with pretty utensils. Did everyone get back on the road safely?"

"They'll be home tomorrow. The wedding went well apparently. And you're not telling me anything. I didn't ask about the weather."

Lex got her in a way the others didn't. She took a deep breath as she searched for the words and realized even if she had them, she couldn't say them without wanting to cry. "I can't right now. I'm coming home day after tomorrow. We'll talk then."

"Okay. Do you need me to do anything to get your house ready for him? Will he move up with a truck or something? A service? Will all his stuff fit into that house?" Lex knew even as he asked, damn him.

"I said I can't right now. I'll see you Wednesday. My love to everyone." She hung up and swallowed back tears.

The others had left by the time she came back. Shane eyed her but said nothing as she sat back down across from him. "I'm sorry. It was Lex."

"Ah." He must have felt she was upset but said nothing about it.

"Are you coming back with me on Wednesday?" She knew she blurted it out but for heaven's sake, how long was she supposed to not ask about the future?

"I have to work this week. I'll come visit soon. Or you can come back here."

She chewed her food, concentrating on the needed calories and not hitting him with her shoe. "So, you envision this like what? Going steady?"

He looked around. "Not here."

Yeah she was done. Not here and not now, apparently.

Standing up, she tossed her napkin down and grabbed her bag. "I'm done. I'll get a cab back to your house."

He moved to stand and she held a hand out.

"You're being ridiculous and making a scene."

"I'm making a scene? I am? You might have a lot more letters after your name than I do but a scene is having a group of people talk around one person no one bothers to even address." She narrowed her eyes at him when he started to interrupt. "It doesn't even matter. I got the point at last. I'm waking up to just what this is and what it isn't." She took a step back and growled in a low voice when he tried to grab her arm, "If you stand up and get near me they'll need to call the paramedics. Leave me alone."

She was proud of the way she stalked out, head held high.

Once she'd gotten back to his house she began to pack. There was no use in pretending. He wasn't going to move to Seattle. He wasn't going to accept who he was, or even who she was. He wanted the glory of fucking a mate but none of the responsibility of belonging to someone. To *something*.

She was a werewolf. Period. Yes, she was his mate and that tied her to him for the rest of her life. But it didn't mean she would tie her life to someone and make them both miserable in the offing. She wanted him to be happy. In the days since she'd laid eyes on him, it'd become inescapable that she loved Shane very much. She knew he thought it too soon and she accepted that he didn't love her the way she did him. She could deal with him needing time to get to know her. But that wasn't what he was asking for.

Perhaps it made her selfish and unfair but she wasn't

going to give up her life, her Pack, her family and who she was to move to Las Vegas and pretend to be everything she wasn't so he could continue to pretend he was human. And then what? She didn't fit into his life. He wasn't shallow. They'd had deep conversations, she knew he volunteered several times a year to man the community health care clinics that tended to lower-income populations. He had a heart, he made her laugh and she liked him when he was being himself.

But he wasn't himself as often as he could have been. As he *should* be. The people at the restaurant she'd met, or rather who patently ignored her, were not what she wanted to be like. Megan loved her life. Loved her connection to who she was and what she did. Trading it for an empty existence far away from her family to be with a man who was afraid of his own identity wasn't what she wanted and she'd certainly not bring children into a family with a dad who would make them hate themselves.

The front door opened and closed. Steps sounded and got closer until he entered the room and halted. She steeled herself, knowing she'd want to fall into him once she saw his face.

"What the hell are you doing?"

"What does it look like?" she asked, tossing her toiletries into the bag.

"You're not supposed to go back until Wednesday."

"No I wasn't."

He grabbed her arm. "Megan, this is stupid. Why? I thought you wanted to get to know me. To take this time together."

"Don't!" She yanked her arm away from him. "I *have* been taking this time. I have been trying to get to know you. I've asked to meet your parents but you want to delay it. I've asked to meet your friends and see where you work but you delay it. And when we do, well, you don't even bother to introduce me to your ex's friends. I've asked to talk about the future but you put me off. I'm trying and you are not. You like to fuck me. That's it. You never should have claimed me if you meant to do this to me." Tears threatened and she hated that weakness but damn it, she didn't want things to be this way. Still, she had no other choice. If she didn't stand tall now, she'd be something she hated and eventually, she'd resent him.

"My mother won't understand! My friends won't understand. You can meet them in a few months when it would make sense for me to be serious about someone. Those people today aren't my friends. They're Cynthia's crowd, young, shallow and stupid. I just wanted them to go away. It was about them, not you. None of this changes who we are to each other. And am I supposed to not like fucking you? I don't hear any complaints when you come four times."

"Your mother won't understand? She's mated to a werewolf. How can she not understand? It's not like werewolves are a secret. How can you not just tell your friends I'm your mate? My whole family knows about you. You haven't told *anyone* about me."

"My friends won't understand. My mother, well, it's complicated. Come on, Megan, cut me a break. I'm a doctor living in the suburbs, not a…"

"Not a wolf?" She wrestled with her outrage, her hurt and humiliation and her need to make things work with him. She sighed, her heart breaking. "I've waited my whole life to find my mate. When we met, I accepted it.

I accepted what you were to me and since you claimed me, I thought you did the same. I know this won't be easy. I know you have issues with being a werewolf, but the bond is in place. You were there when it happened if you recall. But you... I don't know, you're acting like we're going steady or something. Things have changed. Forever."

"I don't know what to say to make you happy. I want you to be happy."

He did, she felt that. That was the thing that made this all so hard. He looked so forlorn she reached out to touch his face, warm and already familiar to her.

"Yes you do." She breathed him in, her system totally attuned to him. Leaving would be terribly difficult. Still, it had to be done unless he was willing to talk. To work it out with her. "Are you ever going to move to Seattle? Are you ever even going to think about it? Will you do the joining ceremony with my Pack, with *our* Pack and run with me? You know it can't work if you stay here and I stay there."

He grabbed her hand, holding it to his cheek. "Then move here. There are werewolves on the police force if you want to work. But you don't have to. Have a life of leisure if you want it. Be here with me. Let me take care of you. Why do you expect me to give up my whole life for you? That's not fair."

She sighed. "It might not be fair. Certainly not from a human perspective. I'm sure you make more money than I do. This house is much bigger than mine. This life—" she indicated the room with a sweep of her hand "—is much more glamorous than mine. I mow my own lawn, I weed my own garden, there's food in my fridge and I let myself get furry and run free and wild as often as I can. But from a wolf's perspective, it's more than fair. Because you don't live as a wolf and I do. I can't, no I won't give up what I am, not even for you, Shane. I can't live a lie. I don't want to be a human. I need to be touched by other wolves. We thrive with that. I wish you'd give it a chance! But you see it as wrong. You see what I am as wrong and I can't live a life where I embrace that. I am not wrong. I am not a monster. I was born the way I was supposed to be and so were you. Your mother is wrong to have done this to you and your father lives a shadow of a life and has let you do the same and for what? Do you think I'd ever allow my children to be ashamed of who they are?"

Sadly, she pulled her hand free and stepped away from him. She grabbed her suitcase and moved to the door but he stepped in the way. "You don't know what you're talking about. You have no right to judge her."

"This is about your mother? At this time you're going to… Fine, let's go there then. I have every right. You gave me that right when you fucked me and claimed me without intending to live up to your end of the bargain. I'm going home because I'd rather live half a life with a mate who refuses to love me being who I am than half a life here, pretending to be what I'm not to claim your crumbs of love."

A horn honked out front.

"My cab is here. You know my number." Kissing him on the cheek she held her tears back only just barely. "I love you. I know you don't love me and I accept that. But I can only be who I am."

He stood there, his back to her, as she walked away. His sadness flowed between them. His anger and frustration too. But her own welled up and swallowed her as she got into that cab and drove away.

She dialed a number.

"I need you. Can you… I need a plane. I need to come home."

Lex simply made it happen and told her he'd see her in a few hours.

Chapter Seven

Lex paced back and forth, Megan knew, annoyed that
Nina had agreed with her and had made him stay at
home instead of picking her up from the airport. She
watched him through the glass briefly before she headed
inside.

She'd needed the time to compose herself after she'd
pretty much cried and cried the whole flight back.

He met her at the top of the stairs, simply putting his
arms around her tight and kissing the top of her head.
All her composure fell away and the tears came back.

"I'm going to have to kill him, aren't I?" His voice
rumbled through his chest and into her body and she
let it comfort her.

"You can kill him again after I do." Nina hugged her
from the other side and Gabby's laugh sounded over the
three of them as she darted into the room and launched
herself toward them.

Megan extricated herself from Lex and Nina to fill
her arms with her niece, who snuggled into her hold and
covered her face with slightly sticky kisses.

"You're home." Gabby looked up at Megan through
wise brown eyes and nodded once, as if that solved the
problem.

"I am. I missed you, Gab."

"I missed you too. Come on, *The Little Mermaid* is on and Mommy made fish sticks and macaroni and cheese for dinner."

Of course to an outsider the conversation wouldn't have been as clear but Megan had been around Gabriella Warden since her very first breath of air and she understood exactly what her niece had said.

"My favorite."

She set Gabby down and allowed herself to be pulled into the family room.

"I'm glad you're home." Nina hugged her shoulders. "Will you stay over tonight and tell us the whole story?"

Megan nodded and allowed them to take care of her.

Shane paced the length of his bedroom and back. Over and over. She'd been gone three days and he felt it in every muscle. Her scent lay upon his sheets, in his bathroom, in wisps of air as he moved through what now felt like a big empty shell of a house.

He wanted to be angry at her. At times he managed it. Usually when he felt like death warmed over at her absence. He resented that physical connection to her as much as he craved feeding it.

At times he vacillated between wanting to call her and never speaking her name again. She hadn't called and it pissed him off. Made him sulky and petulant. Not something he felt very often. Normally if he was this upset he'd call Sid and Layla but he got the feeling Lay would be ready to cut his heart out.

Work had filled his time but once he got home he found himself unable to sleep and so he paced and thought. Not always a good thing. He considered, for a brief moment, calling Cynthia. But in truth, he was married and he had no desire to break his bond with Megan, even as he struggled with his confusion over how to make things between them work.

Just a week before, his life had been relatively simple and now it just wasn't.

A pounding on his front door roused him from his thoughts. He hurried to answer, thinking it might be Megan. Instead it was his father, standing next to Sid.

"You're an idiot. Now let me in."

His father pushed him aside and Sid followed, kicking the door closed.

"Well, hello to you too, Dad. Have a seat, why don't you?" he said as the two men went into the living room and sat. "You want to tell me what this is about?"

His father's eyes widened a moment and then narrowed. Shane couldn't recall ever seeing him this emotional.

"You, boy, sit your ass down and listen up." Those normally calm green eyes sparked dangerously and Shane found himself obeying just because he was fascinated at this side of his father.

"Sid." Shane tipped his chin in greeting to his cousin. "I imagine this has something to do with Megan?"

His cousin just shook his head and leaned back.

"You know, it would be nice to get a call from my only child telling me when he mated! Such an important thing and I have to hear about it secondhand. Secondhand after you've apparently messed it up. I blame myself. I've made mistakes. Mistakes you should learn from right now before you throw away the best thing you'll ever have."

"I didn't know how to tell you. Does Mom know?"

Sid, his normally very laid-back cousin leaned forward and nearly snarled at him, "I can't believe you're worried about that right now. Megan is back in Seattle and Layla is beside herself. The Wardens have drawn a tight circle around her right now and you are public enemy number one. The only thing keeping Lex Warden from showing up here and beating you senseless is Megan threatening to slice him into pieces if he so much as says *boo* to you. What is wrong with you? Shane, why did you claim her if you didn't mean to keep your oath? You feel it don't you? Don't tell me you can't feel her running through your veins, beating in your heart, the breath in your lungs. How can you think of throwing that away? And for what?"

"What your mother feels is beside the point." His father shoved a hand through his hair. "You know she's unhappy. It's who she is and I'm sorry I let it go this far. I love her. She's my mate and I did the best I could, or I thought I was doing the best I could."

"Not that I'm not happy to see you and all, but this is not anyone's business but mine and Megan's. She wants me to give up everything I am to move up there. How fair is that? How much does she *love* me, huh? She wants to change me!"

Sid's wolf bled into his voice. "Bullshit. You want her to stop being a werewolf and pretend to be human. You're the one who wants to change her in a way that is simply impossible. She's not asking you to not be a doctor. She's not asking you to give up your life. She's asking you to let her be what she is. And if you weren't such a selfish asshole you'd see that what she is, is pretty damned important. She's one of the most powerful werewolves in the country. Most of her family, one she's close to, is in Seattle. You don't visit your family, you don't have many friends here. What are you giving up other than your fucking fantasy that you're not a werewolf?"

Ouch. That one hurt. "Selfish? I ask her to wait, to give me some time, and I'm selfish? What the hell has she been saying about me?" Anger and hurt colored his feelings on the matter and he pushed up from the chair to pace.

"When I called her this morning she told me she loved you and respected your choices and not to come over here and interfere," his father said quietly.

"Oh." The anger he'd been clinging to slipped away. Yearning to hear her voice, to feel her skin against his replaced it with such depth he nearly gasped.

"When I claimed your mother I tried for years to get her to accept what I was. She wouldn't. Eventually I gave in because I love her and I wanted her to be happy."

"You did it for her. Is it too much to ask?"

His father hesitated and the emotion, the regret and pain in his voice sliced at Shane. "Yes. In retrospect, yes. I've lived a shadow of a life. I can count the number of times I've run in the last nearly forty years on two hands. I've raised my child without the touch of a Pack. When she punished you the first time you changed and I allowed it, when I helped you to keep it secret... I failed you. I've failed you and I am here because I don't want you to make the same mistakes I did. You *are* a werewolf. You have a mate. It's the greatest gift you'll ever be given until you have children. Do not throw it aside for foolish pride, for your fear of being what you are. You can be a doctor and a werewolf. Be her mate, son. Don't throw this away."

"I can't be what you are. I can't simply give up my life, give it over to her because she won't compromise at all."

Sid stood and looked him over, a sneer on his face. "You're the one not compromising. Cling to your anger, Shane. I hope it keeps you warm at night. She has Adam up there you know. Her Anchor. If I wasn't around and you saw Layla every day and she was hurting, how would you handle it? You can lose her. Don't be stupid and throw her away like this. Adam knows what a catch she is and he's bonded to her as well. Can you live with that? Just tossing her away like she's nothing?" His cousin stormed from the house and his father stopped before him.

"I love you, Shane. You're a good man. A good wolf. You can move up to Seattle and it won't be you giving up everything for her. You know that in here—" his father tapped Shane's chest "—and in here." He tapped Shane's temple. "Every couple has to compromise. Your job is portable, hers isn't. If you truly let yourself feel what it is to be in a Pack, you'll understand asking her to give it up is akin to asking her to cut off her arm. It's part of her in a way you can't begin to understand and for that I am so very sorry. But don't let my mistakes compound yours. Go to her. Be her mate." His father hugged him and then left him to his empty house once again.

He wandered back into his quiet living room and heaved himself onto the couch. He'd never meant to tell Layla and Sid about the first time he'd changed. It wasn't even something he liked to remember but now he couldn't forget it.

When wolves reached puberty and approached their

first transformation, it was harder to control. His father had been helping him quietly, trying to keep it away from his mother who had been taking the changes in Shane very hard.

He'd changed and it had felt remarkable. Joyous. She'd been waiting as he came back into the yard, pulling his shirt on. She knew and she'd pulled him into the house, weeping and railing about how dangerous it was for him to change. How he had to resist the beast within him or risk losing his humanity.

It was a refrain he'd heard many times before but her hysteria, her anger this time had hit home with him. Had settled in his gut, shame, fear of harming her or making her embarrassed for him. He wanted to be the son who got good grades, who made her proud and that son was human.

She'd made him stay around the house for an entire month, giving him long lists of chores from morning until he'd dropped into bed, exhausted well after dark. No Pack had come to help him then. His father had said nothing and so Shane had simply left his wolf behind. Had only let him out when it was unavoidable.

Very few times in his life did he allow himself to celebrate that part of himself, let himself enjoy that tiny rebellion of simply being what his other half was. When he'd accepted Sid's request to be his and Layla's anchor bond and then when he'd scented and claimed Megan.

He sighed and rubbed his eyes, not sure if he could be sorry but not knowing if he could embrace what he'd been taught to hate either.

"Sid did what?" Megan massaged her temples, trying not to take her shitty mood out on her sister. Layla had been leaving messages for a few days and finally just barged into Lex and Nina's, foisting herself on Megan like a limpet. She loved her big sister but Christ on a skateboard, Layla could be an annoying little bulldog sometimes.

"He called his uncle and then they both visited Shane at his place a few days ago. I wanted to go myself but Sid said it would be better if he went with Shane's dad. I wanted to tell you right away but you'd have tried to stop it."

"That's because it's none of your business!" She stood and grabbed her bag. "I spoke to his father a few days ago. He was very nice and all, but of course no one mentioned this little planned visit. And you? You're such a hypocrite. You remember back when you mated with Sid? You ran! Did I run? No. I faced up to it. I asked him to give us a chance. I explained why his moving here was the best option." She hesitated, feeling the now familiar tears but not wanting to shed one more. "I have to go. Adam is meeting me for dinner."

"Don't you care? Don't you want to know what happened? What he said? Does it bother you at all?" Layla got in her face.

"What do you want from me? Because I'm not weeping and throwing myself on the ground, tearing at my hair, I'm unfeeling? Fuck you, Lay. Yes I care. I care so much it breaks me in two every morning when I open my eyes and he's not here. But he isn't. It's his choice. He made the choice to claim me and then not live up to his duty to me. Just like I'm making the choice to live openly as what I am instead of playing human in the desert and cutting myself off from everything else but him. As for what happened." She shrugged and looked around the room. "He's not here. He hasn't called. It's been over a week. I can take an educated guess. It hurts that he's not here but he isn't. I can't make it anything else. So I'll live with the pain because there is nothing else to do."

She stormed out and drove off, annoyed, frustrated and hurt. Over a week and not a damned word. Granted, she hadn't called him either but at that point, she wasn't sure what she could say. The ball was in his court.

She could beg. She would if she thought it would work. She wanted to be with him. Every time she closed her eyes she saw his face. When she got a quiet moment she heard his voice, felt the phantom touch of his lips on her neck.

But if she begged and even succeeded enough to bring him to her, what then? She had to know it was real and not guilt.

Her phone rang just as she arrived at Adam's to pick him up for dinner.

"Megan?" Shane's deep voice slid through her, filled her up in ways that made her achingly aware of how empty she'd been.

"Hi." She sat back in her seat, closing the car door to cut the street noise.

"Can we talk? You know, like every day? I want to... can we try to get to know each other? I can't take the time from work just now but say in two weeks I can come up to visit for a week or so. Would that work?"

She smiled, feeling just a tiny flame of hope kindle in her chest. "Yes. I'd like that a lot. I've missed you. Funny how you can miss someone you barely know."

"Me too. I've missed you I mean. So, what are you doing right now? Wanna talk while I eat my dinner?

We can share a meal." He laughed and things knotted in her gut began to loosen.

"Let me call you back in ten minutes. I'm in my car but I'm only about five minutes away from home and I'll eat my dinner too." She'd beg off dinner with Adam, he'd understand.

"Do you have a webcam? Maybe we could use that and talk. I'd like to see your face."

"Yeah, I do. I'll call you back in a few and we'll get it all set." She hesitated. "Shane? I'm glad you called."

"I'm glad I did too."

When she hung up she jogged to Adam's door. He opened as she approached and pulled her into a hug. His support had helped so much over the last week. He'd accepted whatever her mood had been. Had listened when she wanted to talk, had left her alone when she didn't want to. He'd been more than a friend, he'd filled up at least a small part of the emptiness Shane's absence had created and she'd forever love him for it.

"Hiya, gorgeous. Hungry?" He kissed the top of her head. Another thing was that he'd never been anything more than platonic. Nothing romantic or sexual, just comforting. She could let her guard down with him and he had no idea how much that meant.

"Hey. Listen, I have to bag dinner. I'm sorry. Shane called and he wants to talk. I want to do this. I want it to work."

He tucked a curl behind her ear. "Of course you do, honey. Go on. We can see each other tomorrow or whenever. You know I'm here for you. I'm glad he's coming to his senses. I knew he would."

"That makes one of us." She laughed as she waved and headed back to her car.

"Drive safely! You can't talk to him at all if you get into an accident. Call me later to fill me in on what happens if you want, okay?"

She opened her door and turned back to him. "Thank you, Adam. So much."

Chapter Eight

Shane tried not to be giddy when her image came onto his screen. She was so damned beautiful. More than he'd remembered.

He said so. "Wow, I've missed your face."

She laughed and the sound tightened things in his gut.

"What's for dinner?" She took a sip from a glass and he wished he were there to lick away the bead of glistening liquid on her lip.

He cleared his throat. His yearning for her had been hard to endure but seeing her there, seeing her and hearing her after silence brought it home until his cock ached against his zipper.

"You noticed I don't tend to have food in my fridge. I picked up a chicken on the way home. Got some pasta to go with it and a little cheesecake for after." He grinned. "Not as good as the stuff you cooked when you were here." Nothing was as good as it was when she was with him.

"When you come up, I'll cook for you every day. I promise. I like to cook. My kitchen isn't as huge as yours but it gets the job done. So tell me about your day while I eat this leftover lasagna."

He found himself spilling all the details of his day to her like she was right in the same room. She laughed when he told her about the mix up in his billing, charging him nine hundred million dollars instead of nine hundred. She made a concerned face when he described the difficulty he'd been having with the rest of his practice group in dealing with treating low-income patients.

"I think you'd really like Grace. She's a doctor too and last year she started a walk-in clinic for low-income Pack members in Boston. She really loves the work. She says it's hard for werewolves to get the kind of medical treatment they need because they're often treated like humans, but of course, hello, not so much with the human bio systems."

He agreed actually. He'd seen it a few times and it had driven him nuts. At the same time, her ease in bringing it up when he had such a hard time wrapping his head around it made him uncomfortable.

She sighed. "I've upset you, haven't I? I don't know how to not be straight with you. I don't know how to not just say whatever I feel and share things that are important to me. I'm not trying to push anything on you. I'm just making conversation."

He couldn't lie, the link made it clear just exactly how he was feeling, even so far away. "No. I mean, yes but it's stupid. You're fine." He didn't like the distance in her eyes replacing the warmth she'd had just moments before. "I *want* you to share with me. I'll get over it. So tell me about your day then."

Silly as it was, he liked hearing her recount all her stuff. She spoke of her family with a warmth that filled him with envy. He'd never had that, although he did have a closeness with Layla and Sid, it wasn't anything near what she seemed to share with her siblings and niece.

They spoke for three hours until her eyes began to droop and the sharp need to care for her pounded in his temples.

"Oh, baby, you're looking like you need some rest. Go to sleep. I'll talk to you tomorrow, okay?"

"Wait."

She stood and he watched, mouth gaping open, as she shrugged off her shirt and pants. Her panties and bra followed until all she wore was her creamy skin and a smile.

"Jesus." He had to gulp down water to moisten suddenly dry lips.

Her hands slid up her belly and cupped her breasts. She moaned, low and sexy, and need, sharp and nearly painful, sliced through him.

"So, you know, I've missed you. Like, really missed you." A smile curved her lips and she sat, pushing her chair back enough that he could see most of her body. Especially the way her graceful fingers kneaded and rolled her nipples.

"Are you wet?" he asked as he freed his cock one handed and stroked it lightly.

"Mmm, let me see."

He nearly choked as he watched her fingers slide down her belly and disappear between the lips of her pussy and draw out again, glistening.

"Yes. Yes I am. Talking to you, hearing your voice and seeing your face makes me this way. When I put my fingers up into my pussy it felt so good, Shane. I need to come."

It wasn't like he'd never had phone sex but this was different. He wanted her desperately but he couldn't touch her. He'd have to settle for her touching herself on his behalf while he watched.

"Keep playing with your nipples but put those fingers back in your pussy. I want you to fuck yourself nice and slow for me. Can you do that? Spread your legs wide so I can see everything."

He watched, mesmerized as her fingers slid in and out of her pussy. He heard the wet sounds and the sense memory of her scent came to him, sharp and sudden. He wanted to come too but not until she did. He didn't want anything to take away from the sight of her right there, just beyond his physical reach but his nonetheless.

"Baby, is your clit hard? Swollen and needy? I can remember how it felt against my tongue. The taste of you, the way you got so wet just for me."

Her whimper made his cock jump against his palm and a bead of semen pearled at the tip. He slid his thumb through it, groaning at the sensation, imagining her mouth there instead of his hand.

She held herself open with one hand, displaying the darkened folds of her pussy to him while she fingered her clit with the other hand. She gasped. "Yes, hard and swollen. I need, oh God... I can't stop it."

Her hips bucked against her fingers but her gaze never left the screen, never broke from his.

He stroked his cock. Already just a razor's edge away from climax and it wasn't more than a few breaths before he came, her name on his lips.

She touched her lips with her finger tips. "I love you, Shane. I'll talk to you tomorrow."

"Christ, what a woman," he murmured as she signed off.

It went on like that for a week and a half. Phone or video calls every night when he rushed home from work just to see her or hear her voice. He'd never found himself so willing to disconnect from work before but by three or so each day he'd found himself wrapping up mentally and he'd walked away from his office without looking over his shoulder no later than six.

He *liked* Megan Warden a hell of a lot. She was funny. Fierce in many ways. Intelligent and insightful on top of beautiful and totally self-assured. No other woman compared. God knew he saw hot women by the dozens every day at work or just out and about in town but none of them held his interest at all.

At times he resented that. His loss of attraction for all the women he'd been so interested in just weeks before. But more often, as the calls went on, he began to accept his feelings and attraction to Megan weren't just the bond but that he really did enjoy her company. She'd be a compelling woman no matter what.

He had to see her and she wasn't volunteering to come back to Vegas. Not that he could blame her. She seemed to be going out of her way to let him have the time he needed and he had promised to visit her in Seattle. So he made plans to fly up and spend a week in her territory so to speak.

But he couldn't be gone for a week or two like he wanted because he didn't have the coverage at work and deep down, in truth, he just wasn't sure if he could give her that time in Seattle. Cowardly? Maybe. But he decided to start with three days and four nights to see what happened.

The flight was short enough that he could leave Thursday night after work and arrive in two hours and come back early Monday morning. Enough time to be with her, to touch her and smell her and roll around with her but not too much. He could retreat if he needed to.

He planned to meet her in just a few hours in baggage claim. Funny, sort of full circle from where they'd met before. And then dinner with her family. God knew he was nervous about it but what could he say? She wanted to introduce him to the people who mattered to her. That was important. *He* was important to her, which made him proud.

Chapter Nine

Megan was glad to have the distraction of the two young and handsome men flirting with her at baggage claim as she waited for Shane. Her hands would have been shaking had she not been holding on to her purse so tightly and focusing on being witty while making it clear she was waiting for her special someone.

She felt him before she saw him, but kept on chatting with her admirers. It wasn't about playing a game, but she didn't want to leap on Shane and jump his bones in the middle of the airport. She didn't want to scare him away. The trip was important. He was taking a small step into her life and she obsessed about doing it right.

"Boys, I think you might get your drool all over my wife if you stand so close." Shane's arms encircled her waist and he pulled her back, into the warmth and solid muscle of his body and she nearly groaned aloud at how good it felt.

She turned her head and met his gaze, just as his mouth claimed hers for a kiss. Everything in her melted as she opened for him. He kept her pinned to his body, back to front as he devastated her mouth, took and took and gave in return until she nearly fell over at the overwhelming sensation. *Mine.*

When he let her go, the sounds all around them returned slowly but she never took her gaze from his.

"Hi." She was proud she could speak at that point and the wicked man he was, she saw he knew his effect on her. His smile was smug as well as sexy.

"Hi yourself. You taste good."

She laughed, turning in his arms to wrap hers around his neck. Tiptoeing up, she kissed his nose briefly. "Good. I like to hear these things. God, I missed you."

He squeezed her tight for a moment and she breathed in as he did, their bodies pressed together.

"So who are your friends?" He jerked his head and she remembered the two who'd been flirting with her.

"Oh them? Just a way to keep my mind off how long your flight had been delayed."

They laughed behind her and she felt Shane's jealousy ease through their link.

"You have nothing to worry about."

"Good." He turned a glare on her flirty companions and then tugged her toward the conveyor belt. She waved at them over her shoulder and Shane grunted.

She snuggled into his side as they waited for his bag, just loving being with him after being apart for nearly three weeks. Her wolf did summersaults inside her human skin at his scent.

"How was the flight?"

He kissed the top of her head. "Long. I must have looked at my watch every forty seconds. I thought I'd never get here."

"But you're here now. I'm so glad."

"So we're going to dinner then? At Lex and Nina's house?"

"Don't sound so nervous. Honestly I limited it as

much as I could and Lay helped. It'll just be Lex, Nina, Lay and Sid and my parents. My grandmother harrumphed at me and said she'd see you before the weekend was up. I know you met her briefly before but I can't wait for you to spend some time with her. You'll like her. Or she'll beat you up. My grandmother isn't one to be ignored." She laughed.

She felt his tension ebb a bit as he reached for his bag and pulled up the handle. "Okay. I'm trusting you. And then we have sex, right?"

Grabbing his hand, she tugged him toward the escalators so they could take the skybridge to the parking garage. "Duh. Like a whole lot."

He saw the low-slung, candy-apple-red Mustang and grinned. "Hmm. I suppose I shouldn't be surprised but I expected you to have a truck or something more hardy."

She rolled her eyes as she popped the trunk for him to put his suitcase into. "I'm as hardy as I need to be." Her gaze slowly made the circuit from the tips of his shoes to the top of his head. "If you recall."

He nearly choked as he scrambled to get into the car without his cock popping through his jeans at the visual her comments left him with. Of her below him as he fucked into her body.

"So um, listen, there will most likely be discussion of the binding ceremony tonight. Lex, well, he's very protective of his Pack and his family and he sees you as one of us now. Don't be offended, it's not meant to be that way. He just wants to include you."

Panic rose a moment, until she reached over and took his hand, squeezing it.

"You don't have to do anything you don't want to do."

He felt her melancholy through the link. "Would you like me to do the ceremony?"

"Yes. It would mean a lot to me. But you'd have to run with me. As a wolf."

He hadn't run in three years even though there were times he itched to let his wolf surface. Part of him really wanted to see her as a wolf. His own wolf began to respond and he realized there was an integral bit of his soul he'd walled off.

Really he wanted to talk to Layla about things. But he felt conflicted. She'd been very quiet about the situation and he understood. She was Megan's sister, she had divided loyalties. But in truth, he was very close to her even though they didn't speak all the time. He felt like she knew him better than most anyone else on earth. Maybe that night when he saw her they could talk a bit.

"I'll consider it. I truly will. I am committed to you. I want you to know that. A lot of this stuff is sort of foreign to me so I appreciate your patience as I try to get through it."

She nodded in the twilight reflected through the windshield.

"It's beautiful up here. I remember from the last time I visited. I get to Portland now and again. My aunt lives there." He was babbling he knew but he was so ridiculously happy to be with her.

"I love it. There's so much land around Lex and Nina's place to run in. There's a lake and several ground-fed streams. When you come again for a bit longer, we can go to the hot springs out on the Olympic Peninsula."

"Mmm. You, wet and naked under the stars? I'm so there."

She laughed and he loved the sound.

They made small talk as she described the area they drove through and he asked questions, carefully avoiding werewolf stuff until he felt like an utter tool. She was so careful to not offend him which he appreciated. But at the same time, he didn't want her holding back. Stupid for him to expect to have it both ways and he knew it.

"Here we are," she said as they pulled up a long drive leading up a winding hillside, blanketed with trees. Huge iron gates blocked the way and she pulled to a stop to enter a code.

"Wow, some security system." The gates slid closed behind them and he scented the wildness, the cleanness of the air, the loam of the forest floor not fifteen feet to the edge of the drive.

"We had a scary few years where this was all very necessary. Things have been peaceful for a while now, but I carried a spare magazine with silver bullets for a long time."

He exhaled sharply. He hadn't given it much thought, what she did. But of course she'd have done exactly that. His woman was an Enforcer and he knew enough about werewolf Pack hierarchy to understand just how important her position was to the safety of the Alpha and to the Pack in general. It gave him pause and no small amount of anxiety.

She pulled into a large garage bay and turned to him. "Hey, it's okay now. I'm safe. The war is over. But even if it wasn't, I'm damned good at my job."

Reaching toward her, he grabbed her, bringing her body to his so he could hold her tight as he found his breath. Being separated was hard enough, the thought of her being injured or killed made him nauseated.

"It's the bond. I'm sorry. I know it's intense for you. I take all this for granted, having grown up in this world. I'm Enforcer which means I'm Second. I'm strong enough to hold my spot. No punk-assed wolf or human is going to take me down. I swear to you."

He kissed her forehead before he released her. Resentment began to well within him. It wasn't about the bond, it was that he felt so fucking ill-prepared for all this. It was a part of him as much, if not more than the suburbs and medical school was.

"Nothing for you to be sorry about as long as you're safe. Now, while I'm nauseated, I may as well go inside."

He grinned and she chuckled. "Come on then. Layla and Sid are already here so you'll know a few people and you've met everyone else before, even if was twelve years ago or like for ten minutes in LA."

He didn't freak and run away. That was a step in the right direction. She'd prepared Lex as best she could and Nina would help too. Lex wanted to kick Shane's ass for not just taking responsibility and dealing with the bond, but Nina understood how he felt to a certain extent. Lex could be overprotective and Cade had called four times before she left for the airport. Thank goodness he was on the other side of the country or she'd have a hell of a time keeping them from pinning Shane to the wall.

She led him up into the house and couldn't help but feel proud even as she wanted him to not be nervous. This was her Pack, her family, her home ground and she'd worked hard to be where she was. She wanted him to like it all too.

"Hey everyone!" she called out as they entered near

the family room. Gabby came running and Megan scooped her up into a hug.

"Oh! He's pretty!"

Shane laughed as she turned toward him with Gabby clinging to her like a monkey. "He is, isn't he? Gabby, this is Shane, my mate. Shane, this is Gabriella Warden, my niece."

Shane bowed to them and took Gabby's hand, kissing it. "It's a pleasure to meet you. Your aunt talks about you all the time."

"Don't flatter her too much, she's already nearly impossible to deal with because of how much her father spoils her." Nina came into the room and took Gabby from Megan. "It's nice to see you again, Shane. Welcome and I hope you're hungry. My mother-in-law—" she paused to laugh "—*your* mother-in-law, has invaded my kitchen and has prepared a feast."

"Come on then, brace yourself." Megan looked to him and he kissed her quickly, putting his arm around her waist.

"Go big or go home," Nina called out.

Layla perked up when they came around the corner into the family room but Megan noticed she held herself back from jumping up to approach them. Shane stiffened a bit. Unsure if he should go to Layla? Surprised at seeing her? Megan wasn't sure.

"Go on, it's okay," she murmured to him and nodded at Layla.

Sid approached and enveloped Megan into a hug. "You're so awesome," he said into her ear. "You know it's nothing compared to what he has with you, right?"

"I don't. I mean, I guess. All I have to guide me is

how I feel about Adam. But I know Layla wouldn't do anything to hurt me. Or you for that matter."

Still, she didn't want to look at them. It was difficult, knowing he shared an older bond with her sister, that he'd created a level of trust she didn't have with him yet. She hadn't lied to Sid, she knew Layla would never do anything with Shane outside what was acceptable. It was their intimacy she was jealous of.

"Hey, I haven't seen you in a few days. Don't I get a hug?" Layla called out and Megan turned to her sister with a smile pasted on her face.

Layla noted it, her posture stiffening a bit before she hugged Megan.

"Enough of this stuff. I'd like to meet my new son-in-law!"

Trust her father to cut through the shit. Henri walked into the room with Beth on one side and Lex on the other. Lex's eyes cut to Megan immediately, narrowing a bit as he looked between her and Layla for a brief moment and then swung his gaze to Shane.

"Dad, this is Shane, you remember him I'm sure from when he anchored with Layla and Sid."

Her father shook Shane's hand and then welcomed him to the Pack. She felt Shane's wolf respond to her father's and a rush of lupine energy filled the room. It was exhilarating but Shane looked a bit overwhelmed.

She reached out to squeeze his hand and he clung to her like a lifeline.

"Welcome to Cascadia, Shane. I hope you'll find the land welcoming." Lex shook Shane's hand and then touched his chest over his heart. Tears stung Megan's eyes at the gesture of brotherhood.

"Hey, everyone's here. Sorry I'm late!" Adam walked in and Megan relaxed a bit at his presence.

He walked straight to her and gave her a hug, intuiting just what she needed. Someone who was all about her at the moment with no other motivations.

Adam and Shane did that male clap-back-hug thing they do and everyone headed into the dining room where the table must have been groaning under the weight of four hundred pounds of food.

"Jeez, Mom! There's enough food here to feed a hundred people."

"I figured you'd be so busy over the weekend you'd appreciate the leftovers."

Her mother really rocked sometimes.

"So how are you doing?" Layla asked him as they stood out on the deck overlooking acres upon acres of forest. Megan was off putting Gabby to bed and he suspected, giving him a chance to visit alone with Layla.

"It's a bit overwhelming. She's really close to Lex. I guess I hadn't really understood it until I saw them together. It's um…a bit intimidating I suppose. He doesn't like me much."

Layla put her head on his shoulder. "Of course he likes you. Trust me, if he didn't like you, you'd be in the emergency room right now. But yes, he and Megan are close, they always have been. She keeps him from being too tight-assed. She's very close to Nina and I think is a bit of a calming influence on her. They just want the best for her. They worry that you won't live up to your bond with her."

"And what do you think about it?"

"I think you're scared. This is like a whole foreign

universe to you and you've been raised to be suspicious of it and suddenly you must know the only way to truly be with Megan is to embrace the very thing you've rejected your whole life."

"Not scared really. But you guys can be like a cult. I *have* a life. I resent this 'take it all or leave it' ultimatum I've been given."

She snorted. "You're so full of shit. I'm not as close with Megan as I am with Tee but I know my sister well enough to know she'd never give you an ultimatum like that. But what is it you're asking of her?"

He began to pace, the moonlight on his skin agitating him. "Is it too much to want her there with me? I have a medical practice there! A house. My parents live there. Why should I give that all up to come here?"

"You're the only one who can answer that in the end. You know what she has here and what you're asking her to give up. What she *is*. Who she is. And for what? Can you only be a doctor in Las Vegas?"

"Can she only be a werewolf in Seattle?"

Layla shrugged. "She can't be what she is here in another Pack. Also, she'd have to fight her way up. Do you want that? She'd be challenged again and again and in truth they wouldn't accept her because her mate has repudiated what they are. What sort of life would that be for either of you? Why would you want that for her?" She heaved a big sigh and shook her head. "I'm not going to engage in this with you anymore. If you want to have a serious conversation and you're willing to be totally honest with me and with yourself, let me know. I'm going for a run. The moon is full, can't you feel it pulling your wolf? How long has it been?"

"I'm tired."

"Suit yourself. You know, what would it hurt to give just a tiny bit? To yourself? To her?"

She walked away and he struggled to breathe as his wolf paced inside him. He felt it, his other self, insistent in a way he'd not felt since his early twenties.

He felt Megan coming and tried to compose himself but when he turned, she stood naked in the silvery light of the moon. "Would you like to run with me? The others have headed out on the other side of the property. Gabby is asleep and Hiro is guarding her. It's just you and me out here."

"My God you're beautiful." He brushed his knuckles down her neck and she arched into his touch.

"What does your wolf look like, Shane? Will you show me? Share that with me? You can say no. I'm sorry if I'm coming on so strong. The moon calls and my blood rushes with the tides. I want to feel it with you. So much it hurts to hold my wolf back. But say the word, say no and we can go back to our house."

"I…" He wanted to run. Wanted to feel the wildness course through him once again but the thought of losing his humanity stole his breath.

Her face fell and she nodded. "Come on, let's go home." She turned and walked away and he felt a gulf wider than the nearly twelve hundred miles between Seattle and Las Vegas open between them and it was his fault.

He was falling for Megan Warden. So hard he didn't quite know how to process it. And yet, the issue of who they were and what he felt about it stood between them and he knew it. He just didn't know how to deal with it.

So he showed her how he felt the only way he could.

He loved every inch of her perfect, velvety skin. He showered attention on her body and through that, he hoped she felt what he did.

He loved the way she moved in the kitchen. Smooth, efficient, totally sure about what she'd do next.

"I love the way you do that," he said, smiling. She turned and met his gaze.

"What? Peel potatoes? You're easy."

He stood and moved to her, needing to touch her. It'd stopped freaking him out, the need to be near her, the need to touch her, to smell her skin. It was part of what there was between them and he accepted it. Whether it was a werewolf thing or whatever, it was there and it was real and he was done trying to fight it.

She leaned back into him as he slid his hands over the curve of her shoulders, down her arms, encircling her waist and then back up to cup her breasts.

"Let me love you," he said against the warmth of her neck.

"It's all I want."

He felt the rush of her emotion through their link and it nearly knocked him over. No one had ever been so much to him, had ever connected to him the way she did. The intensity of it roared through him.

Sweeping an arm across the counter to clear it, he picked her up and set her on the edge. Impatient, he made quick work of the frilly tank top she wore and her glorious breasts were at eye level.

"So beautiful," he murmured, licking across the curve of one and then over to the other.

She arched, her fingers sifting through his hair, her scent rising to his nose, drowning him in her and he surrendered, letting himself fall.

Her nipples were hard against his tongue, her moans echoing through her chest. He wanted to give himself to her but he wasn't good enough. She was strong. Sure. Self-assured and confident and he didn't know what the hell he was other than a fool for her. There in Seattle, what was he in comparison to the men she knew?

Her grip tightened and she turned his head to her so she could see his face. "Do not do this to me. Give yourself to me, Shane. Stop holding back. I only want to love you. Can't you feel that?"

"Let me give you what I can."

He pushed her thighs apart and shoved the flimsy skirt she wore up, exposing her bare pussy. God he loved that about her. The way she owned her sexuality so unashamedly. It was a way he felt they really connected, where he could totally be himself without holding back.

His thumbs slid through her wet flesh and she gasped as he manipulated her clit, squeezing just so slightly. He bent, tasting her belly as he moved down to her pussy, her scent and the way she heated against his mouth drawing him to her.

He groaned when his tongue made contact with her, her taste zinging through his senses. She tasted like the best thing ever and he couldn't get enough. Long slow licks, just the way she liked it and just the way he liked to give it to her, pulled her closer to climax.

He didn't want it to end, wanted the quicksilver taste of her pleasure on his tongue, wanted the clutch of her fingers on his shoulders, the squirming against him as she pressed her pussy into his face.

Her nails dug into the hard muscle of his shoulders through his T-shirt and the sound of the cotton giving

way made his cock even harder. The wildness of her,
her strength and nature flavored her body, flowed into
him like magic and for a very brief string of seconds,
he understood what it meant to be a wolf. Accepted it
as he danced fingers and tongue through her sex, drawing her closer to climax.

She cried out as she came, her body arching, stiffening, her emotion and pleasure flowing through the
link and into the room around them. She was everything and more than he'd ever dreamed he'd possess
but even as her orgasm began to die, he felt the space
between them open up again.

He held her like she meant something to him and yet,
it was like she was in bed with a stranger. When they
had sex was the only time she felt truly connected to
him and it wasn't enough. She couldn't settle for that,
a piece of him that was only fleeting. She wanted him,
all of him and he greedily held back. It made her tired.
He made her ashamed, made her hold back when she
wanted to share. She didn't like it. And it made her
deeply sad because the end was there and there wasn't
a thing she could do to make it better.

He'd been with her for three days and he'd avoided
any talk of the joining ceremony. She hadn't bothered
to take him back to Lex and Nina's and he hadn't asked
to go.

She had to face that he didn't want her, not who she
was. He wanted a human woman and she couldn't give
that to him. She wasn't human and damn it, if he loved
her, he wouldn't want her to try and cut out her heart
the way he had.

She knew he wanted to run. She saw it in his face.

But she wouldn't push. How fair would it be for her to do that? He had to come to her and accept not only what she was but what he was too. She had enough issues in her life, living a lie was just beyond the amount of energy she had to expend. And she didn't want to. She didn't want to pass as human.

She'd had hope when he got there Thursday night and now she had none. All she had was the thought of being bound for the rest of her life to a man who didn't love her and never would. She wanted to cry at the unfairness of it all but she'd wait until she was alone.

"Megan, are you all right?" he asked softly.

"Go to sleep. You have an early flight."

"You've been distant since Thursday night. I thought you wanted to try and make this work."

She turned to him. "Don't do this now. Just go to bed."

"Do what?"

Rage suddenly boiled up and she wanted to punch him. "Are you really going to do this now? Because I'm not going to play. If you push me, you're going to get it all. Is that what you want?"

"Of course I want you to talk to me! I wouldn't have asked if I didn't want it."

"Fine. No, I'm not all right. You're a damned liar and I am sick of being your piece of werewolf ass."

He jerked back as if she'd slapped him but she caught the guilty look in his eye and it only made her angrier. "What? What the fuck are you talking about?"

"What wasn't I clear on? You tell me you want to come up to visit. You tell me you want to get to know me but really, all you want is to fuck me. You don't want to know me. You hate what I am and you actually make me feel ashamed. Never in my life has anyone made me feel ashamed of what I am. Until you. You're supposed to love me and you make me feel like a back-alley whore."

"I don't understand. What have I done to make you feel this way? Why would you save this all up until right before I left?"

"What have you done to make me feel any other way? I have tried to be understanding. I have tried to slowly introduce you to my life. But you don't want to know. You don't want to go on hikes. You don't want to meet my friends and family. You don't want to know about my life. You don't want to fit into it at all. Let's be honest, Shane, you don't want me for anything but shoving your dick into. And I let you. I love it when you fuck me so what does that make me? Huh?"

"A woman who likes to have sex with her husband, that's what it makes you! And you don't want to introduce me to your life, you want me to be a card-carrying member of the werewolf party."

"You're not my husband. You are a man ruled by his cock. You claimed me because you were hot to fuck me but you don't talk to me like you talk to Layla. You don't talk to me at all. And you are so fucked up. You *are* a werewolf. *You are a werewolf!* You really should get some help with your denial. And your mother needs to be slapped. Don't bother defending her, I've already had the pleasure of a phone call with her so don't try it."

Confusion, guilt and hurt swamped him, followed by anger and then the last bit of her sentence registered. "You called my mother?"

"Oh for…" She got up and began to get dressed in

short jerky movements. The bitter scent of unshed tears filled the room and he wanted to get on his knees and beg her forgiveness. He'd been a total prick, cold except in bed since she'd brought him back to her house Thursday night. "Your mother called me. Yesterday when you were taking a nap, as it happens."

"Where are you going? You can't just spring this on me and leave." He got up to follow as she left the room.

"To sleep in the guest room. I think it's best. I can't take any more rejection from you without breaking and I don't want to cry anymore."

He wanted to go to her. Wanted to make it okay and yet he stood rooted to the floor, watching his life spiral out of control. "You're not going to walk away from me. Let's work this out. What did my mother say?"

"Ask her yourself, Shane. I'm not her fucking errand girl. She's bat-shit crazy and I am having no part of this mess."

"Please talk to me. How can we fix it if you don't talk to me?"

"Don't do this to me. It's so cruel." She gasped as her tears broke free and began to stream down her face.

"Please, Megan, don't cry." He moved to her but she held a hand out to ward him off. Within him, his wolf pushed harder than he'd ever felt, needing to fix her, needing to comfort her. He fell to his knees with an anguished growl as he fought it.

And her arms were around him, her scent, bittersweet with anguish, pain, love and regret, calmed and soothed even as it made him want to cry himself.

"Let it go. You don't want this. I accept it. I love you so much. You can't possibly know how much. Because I love you, I'm letting you go. The bond is irrevocable,

I can't make it go away but you can be free. I'll arrange to have you driven to the airport tomorrow morning. Don't call me. Just ride out the need and hopefully it'll lessen." She stood up and he heard the door open and close and he was alone.

Chapter Ten

Dully, he drove from the airport back to his house. She hadn't come back the night before and hadn't answered her phone. Layla had come to take him to the airport but had been very closemouthed about where Megan was.

As she dropped him at the airport she'd turned to him. "If you let my sister slip through your fingers you're an idiot. She's the best thing that's ever happened to you. Don't let your fear fuck this up. Is it so bad? To be a werewolf? To accept what you are as well as what she is? Because it's pretty wonderful. It's what I am. What Sid is. What *you* are. Do it, for your sake and for hers. You're so very close to losing her forever. If you don't wise up now, you'll never have a close bond with her. But she has an Anchor, you think about that. And you tell that mother of yours if she ever calls my sister again unless it's to apologize I will fly to Vegas and smack her ass down myself. She's messed your head up big time but I won't allow her to make my sister feel ashamed of what is right and natural. The bond is right, and you know it. It's not too late."

But she wouldn't tell him what his mother had said and he'd gotten out of the car and onto the plane.

His house was empty. Stale. A pretty facade with nothing inside, just like he was.

He went through the motions as the days passed. He tried to call, over and over but she never answered. The ache of her absence burned a hole into him until he literally wanted to howl out his frustration and loneliness.

At first he'd just dug in. Worked fifteen-hour days. Slept when he wasn't working, but the ache, the need of her sizzled through him every moment of the day, interrupted his dreams. He knew he was wrong, knew she was up there alone and he wrestled with going to her.

It was as if he were outside his life, looking in while someone else lived it. Had he always been this damned disconnected? He didn't seem to care about anything. His entire day was shuffling to work, calling Megan and leaving yet more voice mails, trying to get his mother to give him answers and wondering what it would feel like should his fucking life ever get turned on.

"What the fuckety fuck is your issue?" Layla demanded when she called him two weeks later. "Okay so when I was all, *you're gonna lose her* and stuff when I dropped you off at the airport did you think I was practicing lines for some play I was going to be in or what? Shane, what is wrong with you?"

"I don't know! Look, why can't things be easy?"

"Shut the fuck up. Did you just *whine* to me? You, a nearly forty-year-old man. A successful doctor, a man with a hella amazing wife who is broken into pieces over his seeming lack of emotion where she is concerned. You have *everything* and you're pissing it away to live alone with human women who occupy your bed for twenty minutes and no friends and no real connection to your family? And look at me! You're making me talk in italics and stuff. You know how I hate that. Why are you not here?"

He actually wanted to laugh for the first time in weeks. God he had so missed Layla, and talking to her just made him miss Megan even more and the laugh died away. "There are no other women. I wouldn't do that to her. Anyway, she told me to go."

"So, you want to guess who came to dinner at Lex and Nina's on Sunday with Megan? Adam. Yeah, he's being a very good friend right now. An Anchor. Of course Megan just walks around with dead eyes and her skin looks like hell and she doesn't see the way Adam looks at her. But I do and you're a damned fool. Get over your childhood already. Stop acting like you're starring in a Woody Allen movie. Put on your big-girl panties and get up here. If you don't I will beat you. Dumbass. Sid sends his love."

She hung up before he could argue and he put his phone down with a long sigh. Woody Allen movie indeed. What did she know about it? Her and her damned perfect family.

He had to get out of the house and he needed to eat so he headed to a diner on the outskirts of town. Away from the lights and the tourists. This was old-world Vegas where the food was cheap, came in heaping portions and the waitresses called him *sugar* and put an extra scoop of vanilla on his warmed apple pie.

"Hey there! It's Doctor Shane Rosario." Gina, the woman who'd been serving up his pot roast and slice of pie for as long as he could remember, winked at him as he came in.

He kissed her cheek and she squeezed his arm. "The

usual? Although we got some cherry pie tonight, better than the apple."

"Okay, I trust you."

As he sat and looked out at the waning light fading from the bruise-purple sky, he opened himself up and took a look. Not pretty. Sort of wussy for a man who'd always prided himself on doing the grown-up thing.

He looked out over the restaurant after his food arrived, taking in the clientele ranging from twentysomething, pierced punk rock emo kids to old guys with sandals and socks.

"You okay?" Gina propped a hip on the edge of the booth across from him. "You look down tonight."

"How's your husband, Gina? Last time I was in he'd had some problems with his diabetes."

She smiled. "Aww, such a good boy you are! Thanks for asking. Don is good. His medication is working and he's finally taking care of his diet. Him and the sneaking off to eat junk! But you know, in the big picture he chose me over lots of bread and potatoes and boxed food. I'd rather have him alive and with me than not. Thank goodness he feels the same."

Her husband was a retired air force pilot. She'd worked as a waitress at the Silver Dollar since his dad had first brought Shane there for pie when he was nine or ten years old. They had kids a bit older than Shane. Her husband, Don, had developed type-two diabetes and had been in and out of the hospital as they'd tried to get it under control.

"That's good to hear. You know, I met someone. Married her. I hope someday I can have as many years under my belt with her as you and Don do."

She laughed. "Oh that's wonderful news! You two

fighting? Is that why the long face? Let me give you some advice, doctor. Love isn't enough. Love isn't enough so you have to work your tail off to make up that last twenty percent. Don't rely on love, rely on your head and your heart and the knowledge that working and being in love is way better than slacking off and having it all fall apart later. Some people are doormats, that's not working love. But some people expect the other person to just drop everything. What do you want? What do you want together? Once you know that and once you're both working on the same team, you're unbeatable."

Love wasn't everything or she'd be there with him now, having given up her entire life to be his wife. And if he really loved her, would he want her to do that?

"Your kids are lucky to have you and Don as an example."

She shrugged. "We had our moments. Our thin times. People make mistakes, sometimes big ones that hurt. Sometimes you can forgive but forgetting is another thing. But I love that man and he loves me enough to give up all those carbs and refined sugars." Squeezing his shoulder, she dropped off the check. "You be sure you work hard for this girl. And bring her around here so I can check her out. I'm off shift and I need to get home or I'd stay to hear all about her. You come back in here soon, you got me?"

He nodded. "Tell everyone I said hello."

"You tell your daddy the same."

Dropping the money on the table, he headed out. Was he supposed to go to therapy now? Have someone tell him his mother issues keep him from having a real relationship with…holy shit, he *was* acting as if he was starring in a Woody Allen movie. He wanted to kick his own ass.

Yes, his mother was the source of a lot of this but so was his father and he was way past the age where he could be blaming his damned parents for being an idiot.

Since his mother doggedly refused to answer his questions about her discussion with Megan, he finally drove over to his parents' house to demand answers. He needed to move forward in his life.

His mother waited at the door for him as he approached. "It's about time you showed your face around here. You have something to tell me, don't you?"

He opened the screen door and dropped a kiss on her cheek before going into the house. The house he'd grown up in and had always *felt* like he should appreciate but one he was relieved to move out of for college and medical school.

"I hear tell you've had a little chat with my wife and I thought I'd see just exactly what you said to her since you wouldn't tell me over the phone. I figured Dad would have told you about me and Megan."

His father sat in his favorite easy chair, near the big picture window looking over the wildness just a few blocks away. Shane suddenly got it and part of him ached for his father while another part raged.

"Don't expect me to do your work for you, boy. Anyway, what exactly would I be telling her?"

"Hey, Dad." He paused to kiss his dad's temple and a bloom of emotion unfurled, comfort, he realized and wondered if it had to do with a father-son thing or a werewolf thing. God he was messed up.

Tension thickened the air in the room though. Expec-

tancy hung heavy and he realized it was all the avoid-
ance he'd built up over the past month.

"I'm glad you're here, Shane, and I hope you're here
to tell us you're moving to Seattle to be a husband to
your mate? Or is it that you chose the easy route of self-
loathing and stayed here while your beautiful Megan
floundered? What will you feel when she finally gives
up and finds some measure of happiness with another
man?"

He looked at his father, hurt stinging his eyes and
all the words that had built up over his lifetime threatening to explode.

"That's rich coming from you!"

His dad heaved a sigh. "It is."

"Enough! So you went to Seattle to see her then? Did
you turn furry at her beck and call?"

He turned slowly at the verbal slap. "What did you
say to her?" He tried to keep his temper down. She often
made him antsy, made him feel his skin fit all wrong.

"What did she tell you I said? I imagine it was quite
a tale. Her kind doesn't seem to know her place." The
bitterness in his mother's voice cut at him. Why was
she so unhappy?

"Haven't we done enough to mess with him, Sheila?
He has the chance to be happy, why can't we unite to
help him? And if you recall, I'm her kind. Your son is
her kind." His father rarely engaged with her but anger
flashed in his eyes just then. "Why don't you tell us
both what you said to the girl?"

"Mess with him? By keeping him away from that
world and grounding him in one where there are no
monsters? We did what was best. You and I agreed! As
for the girl as you call her? I told her she wasn't good

enough for him and she isn't! This chemical mumbo jumbo makes him want to rut on her but that's all it is. Sex. He can't love her. She's a monster. I told her she'd make his life a hell unless she gave up being a werewolf like you did." She turned back to Shane. "He did it for me and she could do it for you if she wanted to. But she won't because she's an animal. You're better than that. I was just saying what had to be said. I love you and I want what's best for you. If you wanted this girl you wouldn't be here, you'd be there. That's proof enough."

And it hit him then. Hard. God, she was right. He'd been dancing around this crap and it was right in his face.

"How can you look at him for forty-three years and think he's a monster?" Shane turned to his father who'd moved to stand. "And you? Packless. How? Why? Don't you miss your people? Your family?"

"I love her. I loved her then and I love her now and she was so afraid. So I got caught up in it and I thought it was best because it made her happy but now I look at it, at you, our beautiful son, and I see we both failed. You are not a monster. Neither is Megan. The mate bond is something miraculous. You're not bound to her to your detriment, it makes you better. You are a were-wolf. She is a werewolf. So strong your woman. She has a Pack who will take you in, shelter you, give you the connection you need. Take it! Don't hide from what you are because I did you wrong. I'm sorry. I love you, Shane, and I want you to be happy. You can't be happy if you deny what you are."

"We've had a good life. I don't know how you can pretend we didn't." His mother looked back and forth between them. "We did what was best. Your people wanted him to run and turn into an animal. She is like that. It's what she does…" Her voice trailed off and her hands fell to her side.

"Go to her. What do you have here? A big empty house? You can be a doctor there too. Megan is there. Don't you want to be with her? Live in a Pack? You have no idea the amazing future you have awaiting you. If you only take the courage to grab it." His father hugged him and comfort bloomed again.

"Thank you, Dad. I have to go." He turned and his mother grabbed his arm.

"I did it because I love you."

"I know you do. But I am what she is too. What Dad is and I have to find a way to make this work because I love her. I've been spending so much time denying what I am that I lost sight of that. I have to go. If you call her again I won't protect you from a whole bunch of pissed-off Warden wolves." He hugged her and jogged to his car.

What a fool he'd been.

He dialed Layla and Sid's house and got the machine. He dialed Megan but got her damned voice mail. He called Lex and Nina's and finally got someone to answer.

"Nina, this is Shane. Is Megan there?"

"Shane who? I don't know any Shane." Nina's voice was dry but the hostility came through loud and clear.

"Okay okay so I deserve that. But I'm trying to make things right. Can I talk to her?" He narrowly missed rear-ending a semitruck.

"She's not here. She and Adam are out at the coast for the weekend." And she hung up.

The coast? What the hell? It didn't matter. He had

work to do and a woman to really claim. He'd deal with whatever the hell was going on when he arrived.

She needed the distraction. Megan lay in the sun, the sound of the water soothing jangled nerves as she tried to nap. Unsuccessfully.

She'd never had trouble sleeping before but damn if she wasn't resorting to the herbal teas her grandmother made to try and get some rest. She missed him and his calls didn't help her resolve to let him go. Damn it.

Her muscles hurt, her head hurt and she wanted him. She wanted to smell him on her skin, to feel him against her body at night. She wanted to make him pancakes and bacon in the mornings and listen to the rumble of his voice through the wall of his chest as she sat snuggled against him.

It was unfair, that's what it was. Unfair. Why couldn't he love her enough? He was so incredible, so sexy and intelligent and truly caring but he just couldn't give over enough.

Gah! Speaking of unfair, that's what she was being. She knew it was way more complicated than him not loving her enough. In truth, her heart hurt for him because he was raised to fear and hate what he was. Where she was raised to love herself and her roots, he was raised to be ashamed. It was a wonder he was as strong and good a man as he was after the job his mother did on him. And his father too, she supposed. Her father went on runs with her once every two weeks, just to be with her. His father, from what she understood, had to hide his behavior as a wolf, if he ran at all.

It was unimaginable to her, to be estranged from your own wolf, your identity! To not be close to your family. To not have the comfort of a Pack. She wanted that for Shane, knew it would help heal some of his hurts but he was afraid.

She'd been with Adam the night before. He'd listened to her cry, handed her tissues and at the end, he'd told her she had to make some choices about where she planned to go.

"You can keep this up and slowly fade away. You can fight for him, force him to see what he's missing. Or you can let go, accept he won't ever come to you and move on. I'm here for you no matter what, I love you. But you cannot go on this way." He'd kissed her on the top of her head, tucked her hair behind her ear and had gone.

His words echoed in her head as she pondered her options for the millionth time but just could not truly consider letting go.

"You're thinking about him again."

She cracked an eye open to find Nina leaning down, holding out a glass of iced tea.

"What of it? Are you the thought patrol?"

"Don't try to out-bitch the master." Nina stretched out next to her on a chaise lounge. "Just because you saved my life a few dozen times doesn't give you the right to be snippy with me."

Megan rolled her eyes and sipped her tea. "Living with your bitchy ass has given me a lifetime pass. I can't believe you told him I was at the coast with Adam."

"Look, okay yeah so I'll give you the living with me means you can be snippy point. Like a thousand times more than you are. Thank God you're the calm Warden, that's all I can say. Well no—" Nina laughed "—I can say loads more, but you know what I mean. Anyhoodle, he needed to realize he could lose you. You have an Anchor. Adam would love to step into Shane's place. Anyway, you're at poolside with me, close enough. Your man needs to suck it up and deal. Good lord, look at you! If I was into girls I'd be all over you and stuff."

Megan choked on her tea a moment. "Um, thanks. Back atcha. But Adam isn't like that! And also, you know he could be here now, Shane that is, and he's not. So apparently he wasn't that shaken up by the idea of me canoodling with Adam at the shore."

"*Canoodling* is such a weird word. Who made that shit up anyway?"

"Focus! Everyone keeps saying stuff about Adam and it's pissing me off. He has never made a single romantic advance toward me. He has encouraged me over and over to fight for Shane. He's an honorable wolf and he's my friend." She growled and took a sip of her tea. "Anyway, you said *anyhoodle*, that's sort of a connected term in some sense isn't it?"

"Now who needs to focus?"

She laughed. "You're a bad influence on me. Don't you have a husband to torment or something?"

"He's off with Gabby and your dad. Daddy and Grandpa all day long, she's going to be hell to get to bed tonight. Hey, let's go out for dinner or something so I don't have to do it." Nina grabbed her hand and squeezed and that meant so much. Nina knew her so well, knew how tormented she was and was there for her.

"I'm having dinner with Adam at The Dahlia Lounge. Come with us. The whole gang will be there. Then Hiro can be on Gabby duty with Lex and my dad."

"Okay. Let's go now so Lex can't give me those

damned eyes of his. You know the ones that resulted in Gabby's existence to begin with."

"Ew."

"Don't knock it. Hey, let's call Layla too. Come on, Megan, she wants you to confide in her. She feels so lost right now."

Megan got up and pulled her T-shirt on and slid into her sandals. "Fine."

"You two are both stupid. She loves you." Nina got up and followed her through the house, pausing to call Lex and tell him they were going to dinner.

"I never said she didn't love me. Again with all that assumption. Lay and I talk every day I'll have you know. She and I are fine, we worked through this mess, or the best we could. And this time when you borrow my stuff you have to give it back."

"You love my quirky ways. Admit it." Nina smirked as she belted in and Megan pulled down the long drive.

"I admit no such thing. You stretch out my shoes, your child gets cereal bar gunk on my clothes and there are so many Cheerios and Goldfish in my seats I could live for a week if I got stranded. Your husband has put me in charge of your safety and you're a magnet for trouble. You're unbearably nosy, you have horrible taste in music and you eat marshmallow Peeps, which are disgusting."

"Like I said, you love my quirky ways. And all the more Peeps for me, bitch. Shut up with the whining now so I can call Layla."

Nina dialed and made arrangements while Megan tried to not think about any of this shit and failed.

Chapter Eleven

Tired but still running on the adrenaline of finally making a decision, Shane pulled into the driveway. Her car was there and when he opened the door, he heard the low rumble of music from inside.

On the porch, his bag slipped from his fingers as he caught sight of her, curled up in a chair, looking out her back window. Ani DiFranco's "Grey" played on her stereo and the immense wall of her sadness swept him up and nearly knocked him to his knees.

He whispered her name and she turned toward the front window next to her door and saw him. Her eyes were reddened and he knew he was the reason.

She shook her head and he tapped three times. "Please, please open the door."

She stood and his heart slowed a moment as he took in how bad she looked. Her eyes were swollen, and dark smudges marked just below. Still, she was the most beautiful thing he'd ever seen.

"Please."

She took a deep breath and moved to the door, standing in it to block his access.

"What are you doing here?" Tears thickened her

voice, cut to his heart, and his own blurred his vision just a moment.

If I lay here, if I just lay here, would you lie with me and just forget the world?

The track changed from Ani to Snow Patrol.

"It's like the mixtape of our relationship." He ate up every detail of her face, even the tears.

"I can't see you, Shane. It's too much. Don't make me tell you to leave again. It was hard enough the first time." She took a step back but he reached out, cupped her cheek and she halted, leaning into his touch. Her breath hitched and he thumbed away her tears.

"Oh, baby, I'm so sorry. Give me a chance. A real one. Will you help me? Help me be a wolf? Help me accept us both?"

"All that I am, all that I ever was… I want to love you but you've hurt me. I'm afraid if I let you in again you'll destroy me."

He fell to his knees and buried his face against her belly. Her scent surrounded him, buffeted him, made him all right. Her fingers slid through his hair, against his scalp, down his neck.

She sighed and he felt her resistance melt, and re-solved to do whatever it took to make things right. To love her the way she was meant to be loved instead of the way he'd made her feel until then.

"Open yourself then. To me. Come inside and let me touch you and your wolf."

Overjoyed and awed by her strength, he stood on shaky legs and grabbed his bag.

"If you come through this door, you're going to do this right? Because honestly I can't take it if you re-ject me."

He kissed her, softly, just a breath of his lips against hers. "I'm fucking freaked out, but I trust you. I can't promise it'll be easy but I want to do this and I want you to help me. I just don't know how."

"Come on then. Let me show you."

Her hands shook as she closed the door and locked it. "Come in. Why don't you put your bag over there." She indicated a space next to her couch. She wasn't ready to invite him to unload in the bedroom yet.

He did and turned to her. "I am so sorry. I…" He shrugged and she knew. She understood. But knowing didn't mean she was ready to just let him hurt her again. She had to be sure he was ready to stand at her side.

She touched him, his energy vibrated through his skin, his muscles taut against her palm. "Let's take this one step at a time, all right?"

They sat and he pulled her to him, holding her, breathing her in and she relaxed, needing the contact as much as he did.

"Why are you here? Now instead of two weeks ago?"

"Let me go back more okay? When I met you, when I claimed you, I wanted you. It wasn't just about fucking you, no matter what you think. I let my wolf take over in a way I hadn't in many years, not more than a handful of times over my life. But then, okay so you came to my house and you held a mirror up to me and it sucked. You're this fully formed person! I am not. I couldn't handle it. So I pushed you away and then you left and I should have stopped you then but I didn't. And then my dad and Sid came to me and they said a lot of stuff that made sense and it gave me an excuse to finally reach out and call you and then of course I got to know you and the more I got to know you, the more I fell for you."

She wanted to interrupt, to tell him he was fully formed but being stupid, but instead she let him talk. The way he rushed through his sentences told her if she interrupted he'd never get out what he needed to say.

So she threaded her fingers through his and let him talk.

"And I came up here and you were just so *vivid*. So full of life and so self-assured. You move with purpose, Megan. You take everything head on and that is so amazing, so sexy. I'm in awe of it. That night when you wanted to run with me? I wanted to so badly but I couldn't get it out of my head. My foreignness. What if I did it wrong? What if you were better at it than I was? What if you were disgusted by me?"

He paused and she heard him swallow. She ached for him, wanted to shake his mother and show her what she'd done to her child.

"And so I opened myself to you the only way I felt I could and still be good at it. I don't know! When we were together in bed, I felt like we were totally connected but now I see you must have felt used, like it's all I cared about. But that's not how it was. Not how it is.

"Back in Vegas I went to my parents' house, a few days ago, and I confronted my mother about her call to you. When she told me what she'd said, I, my God, I didn't know what to do or say to her. My father apologized for the way I was raised and urged me to come to you. I left and did some planning. But I went back to him the next day and we ran. As wolves. The last time we did that I was twenty-two! He apologized for not being a stronger force in my life, offered to come up here with me to help."

"If I ask you to run with me right now, would you?" She turned to look him in the eye.

"Yes. I'd... I'll admit I'm worried but yes, I would. I will. I want to have this with you. Do you think I want to hate what I am?"

She shook her head. "I hope not. I love what you are. We can go slow. You ran with your father, that's awesome. I want that with you. It's important to me, I won't lie. But we can take little steps. However, I can't do this long-distance thing. I just can't. All cards on the table, I want a mate. I want a husband at my side. You don't have to come to Pack gatherings and do all the wolf stuff if it makes you uncomfortable but I am a werewolf and I am one openly. I want children, I won't raise them to fear what they are."

"I made some calls over the last several days. I'm going to apply for my license to practice up here. I have some friends from medical school and Grace said she'd help me too. You were right, I did like her. She's very much your advocate." He grimaced. "She schooled me a bit on you. And then today, Nina, man oh man! She chewed me up and spit me out before she finally told me you weren't at the coast at all but here. Anyway, I want to be here with you. I want to be your husband. I've never been in a Pack before. I'm not even particularly close to my family so I can't promise it's going to be smooth or easy but I want to try."

"Why? Why now? Two weeks ago you didn't. Two weeks before that you didn't. Why now?"

"I've tried living without you and it sucks. I *like* you, Megan. And what's more, I love you. The more I thought about you, about what we could have, the more I thought about what I didn't have. I don't have a full life, I do when I'm with you. And you know, Layla and my father and you too, you all served me some harsh truths about how I was raised and who I was taught to be. I'm choosing to not hate myself. I can be that with you. At your side I can be who I am. Or you make me want to work at it, at the very least."

For long moments she opened herself to their link. Letting herself feel just what he was saying openly and fully. She hadn't done it since they first made the bond and he rushed through her, dizzying her, making her slightly drunk with him.

Hope burst through her from the dying embers of just an hour before. And then desire.

"Megan?" His pupils nearly swallowed all the color in his eyes. "I know you felt like I was just using you for sex before and I'm sorry. But I'd love to…fuck, I'm dying to be inside you. I've been thinking of you non-stop, you know? Not just of you naked and beneath me but of your voice, the way your hair catches the light. Everything. But I can't deny I don't love to be with you naked and sweaty."

She stood and held a hand out. "Come on, I just put new sheets on the bed and the air conditioner is on in there. Let's get sweaty."

The room was cool and the curtains had been drawn so it was dark, a refuge from the outside world. Even in the dark he could see her clearly as she reached to turn on a small bedside lamp.

Without words she crossed the room and drew him closer to the bed. Slowly, she pulled his shirt up and over his head, her mouth leaving wet, hot kisses across his chest. Every place she touched burned, tingled with the electricity of their bond.

He groaned, wanting her more, needing to crawl into her, taking refuge, being one with her in a way he'd craved since the very first moment he saw her at LAX. She called to him physically and emotionally from the start. It was more than the bond, it was simply her.

"I love how you look. You're so masculine, so handsome and strong." Her lips moved against the sensitive skin of his neck as her hands smoothed down his back and grabbed hold of his ass, pulling him closer.

"You're going to kill me," he moaned.

"You'll die happy," she murmured as she dropped to her knees and unzipped his jeans.

All the blood in his body rushed away from his head and straight to his cock as she pulled it free from his boxers. Eagerly, he kicked out of the pants and underwear, standing totally naked in front of her as she knelt.

Beautiful.

Slowly, agonizingly slowly, she leaned in and slid her tongue through the slick bead of pre-come on the head of his cock. Zings of sensation arced through him at the wet heat of her mouth as she surrounded his cock with it.

He braced his knees as she continued to suck him all the way in and then pull back, her fingers doing amazing things to his balls as she worked. Over and over and over again until he couldn't feel anything but that, the pleasure of it, of all her attention being on him. He nearly lost it, had nearly given up on this? He was ten kinds of fool.

She hummed, a deep sound of arousal around his cock and it vibrated up his spine, right to his brain.

"Christ!" he hissed as she sucked very hard and dug the tip of her tongue into that nerve-laden sweet spot just below the head. And before he could say anything else he came hard, so hard he saw stars paint his vision as it felt like his whole body rushed out the head of his cock, filling her with him.

He thought he would fall boneless to her bed until she pulled her mouth back, looked up into his face and licked her lips. It was round two and right then, as he picked her up by the upper arms and kissed her, hard.

His mouth never left hers even as his hands tore at her clothes, sending them all over the place until she was as naked as he. His hands were everywhere at once, kneading, stroking, pinching and, *ahhh* his hand slid between her thighs, finding her clit. Her hips jutted forward of their own accord.

He made a sound, laced with need and want and pleasure. She swallowed it eagerly. He'd come to her, really come to her. Feeling him now, the difference was palpable. There was nothing between them anymore. Every nerve ending in her body sang as he loved her. Miraculous. Nothing in her life had prepared her for this onslaught of sensation. It marked her, changed her utterly.

Her eyes fluttered open as she lost his body heat when he pulled away. His smile was wicked. "Don't look so alarmed, I want to lick you. Everywhere."

"Oh. Well, I like that idea." Simply forming a smile took so much effort when all she wanted was his hands and mouth on her again.

She liked it even more when he lay down. He was a big, chiseled hunk of man there and she wanted to take a big bite.

"Come on up here." He indicated she straddle his chest but she stood and looked at him some more.

"I really like looking at you this way. I really think this is what I should see every time I come home."

He smiled. "I'll do my very best to make that happen. Now, pardon my crudity but I want to taste your pussy and I can't do it unless it's right here above my face."

Whoa. She shivered. "You should be illegal in thirty states," she managed to stammer. She hadn't felt this bowled over by him before. Turned on, yes, but he was just so overwhelming right then.

Not so overwhelming she was unable to move up and position herself the way he suggested with a waggle of his brows. Broad, strong hands smoothed up the outside of her thighs.

"You might want to hold on to the headboard," he said right before he grabbed her hips and pulled her to his mouth. His mouth, sweet heavens, that mouth of his went to work with lips and tongue and the slight scrape of teeth. Devastating, taking over, filling her with nothing but the memory of the way he loved her.

The tip of his tongue flicked and danced against her clit in just the right way. His fingers, digging into the muscle of her thighs and ass, held her just where he wanted so her only option was to grip the headboard and let him do his work.

Closer and closer he drew her in, every few long moments he'd change up, stab his tongue deep into her body or suck just so lightly on her clit. Build it into the overall rhythm until she hurtled toward orgasm so fast and so hard her entire body seized as she hissed out his name.

But he kept on, on and on, relentless until she tipped,

hard, into another orgasm on the heels of the first, this one rendering her thigh muscles to burning, useless blobs. Before she collapsed, he flipped her onto her back and moved up her body, even as her pussy continued to spasm, seeking to be filled.

And he answered that need in one hard thrust as he held her open, keeping her thigh up at his waist. Thick, wet sounds filled the room, buffeted by indrawn breath and the frenzied meeting of flesh.

Need crawled through her veins, craving for him, for the man she was fated to belong to forever, the man she'd been born to love and be loved by. What a momentous thing it was to be with him, truly, completely with him as he pressed into her and withdrew all but the very tip of his cock, on and on.

In the course of a single day she'd moved from desolation and terrible loneliness to the sort of completeness she'd heard her sisters talk about but truly doubted she'd ever had lodged within her.

Her hands needed to touch every inch of his skin she could reach, needed to hear the way his breath changed as she did something he really liked. His skin broke into gooseflesh as she dragged her nails up his sides, his pupils enlarged and his breath caught. His nipples pebbled as she arched up to lick over one and then the other.

"God that feels good."

She nipped at the sensitive skin before looking up at him. "You're not doing so badly yourself."

"I love you and I'm sorry I hurt you."

Swallowing her emotion, she smiled and rolled her hips. "I have waited since the first moment you touched me for you to truly accept me and what this is."

"I don't deserve you. But I'm keeping you anyway.

The bond saves my worthless ass from being tossed out onto the street." He laughed as he thrust, changing his angle and dragging the entire line of his cock over her sensitized clit. She writhed against him with a sharp intake of breath.

"That's right, your pussy feels so good around me like this. You're so damned right. Beautiful. *Mine*."

And it hit her, the feeling she'd been so hard pressed to define? It was that she belonged to him, truly and completely. How amazing was that? Tears welled in her eyes and the pain released, unfurling from a tight ball deep within her. She wept even as he made her come again, even as he came while raining kisses over her face, tasting her tears, whispering her name and that he loved her.

Deep gulping sobs wracked her entire body, every part of her released the grief stored within every cell. And he held her through it all, held her as she cried the pain away, replacing it with love, replacing it with understanding and caring, and he did not leave. He stayed there, still half inside her body, his own sheltering her as he did not hide from what he'd created, from what they'd created together.

And when she was done it was as if a switch had been thrown. She sniffled her last and looked up at him. He wore a half smile, his brow still etched with concern. "I can say I'm sorry again but it can't make up for what you just went through."

She touched his face as he fell to the side, still holding her. "No more of that. It's over. This is day one and we can only move forward."

Chapter Twelve

She looked at him, her wolf, her mate as he lay on his side, breath heaving from their run up the side of the hill. The small patch of white on his front leg pleased her as much as the glint of sharp white teeth.

The earth welcomed them as they'd run, welcomed them each night as they slipped their human skin and let warm loam and fresh pine crush beneath footpads. He howled, answered in the distance by another of their Pack. The strength of such unity rang through her, made her feel welcomed and safe, fiercely protective and proud.

Things were good. And right. The life within her stirred, the human flared, reminding the wolf of that other time when she lived within instead of on the outside. Her mate looked to her and stood. Nudging her, pushing her back to that place with the bright lights.

Shane watched as she found her human skin again. The swell of her once flat belly brought joy to him, their child grew there. After two years together, they'd created a baby, a baby he'd hold in his arms in just three months.

"You all right?" He kissed her temple as he handed her the fleece hooded sweatshirt.

She smiled, leaning into his body. "Yes, of course. Just a bit tired. Gestating is a tough job."

"If you hadn't insisted on weeding the entire back garden with Gabby and Nina you probably wouldn't be so tired." He laughed as they made their way back to the house just a few feet away.

Off in the distance, Lex and Nina's place peeked through the trees. Their own house had been finished for about a year. His entrance into Cascadia had been slow but solid. Lex was overbearing and nosy but he loved his sister and as Shane did too, over time, the two of them built a solid friendship.

Layla and Sid were already on the back deck, holding out mugs of hot chocolate. Megan took hers and looked to Shane and rolled her eyes. "Go on. I'll see you later."

"You are so awesome." He kissed her soundly and she laughed. Before he went off with his cousin to watch the movies he'd brought over, he caressed the bump on his wife's belly and the corresponding squirm and kick against his palm made him look into her face again. "You are. I adore you. There isn't a moment during my day when I don't discover some new way to love you."

Her amused look softened and she took his face in her hands. "Once I snared you, I wasn't letting go. Now don't eat too much popcorn."

He left, satisfied, knowing his life only got better every day.

"You okay?" Layla pushed the footstool over so she could put her feet up.

"Absolutely okay. They looked like seven-year-olds running off to catch frogs or something."

Layla laughed. "They did. How many times did Lex call you today?"

"Four. Mom called five. You called twice, Tracy once, Tegan once and Grace twice. Grandma just stopped by."

"We worry."

"I know. It's very sweet. Until the third call. But you know, that's the breaks. We called Tee this many times and Tracy too. Nina doesn't answer the phone now with the baby and Gabby running riot but she got the calls and visits. It's weird to not be up there all the time now."

"It was time. The Enforcer's job doesn't have to be a full-time guard to the Alpha. Anyway, Hiro is so good at it and he can take Nina without even blushing. You need to keep yourself on the special diet and try not to be stressed."

"I love you." She reached out and squeezed Layla's hand.

"I'm so glad we have each other. I was worried but he came through thank goodness."

"He comes through every day. It's like that first month didn't even exist. Every once in a while, I look at him and try to imagine what it would be like if he'd never come to me." She shrugged. "But I can't. Because he's been so solidly here ever since."

"Sometimes you try to fight what's fated but hell, you can't fight fate, cookie."

"Who wants to when fate drops tall, dark and handsome into your lap?"

"Yes, those Rosario genes are pretty impressive."

"Hey you two!"

They turned to see Nina come up the walk, wearing the sling.

She kissed each of them and sat, patting the bundle slowly. "He's been sort of cranky. I thought a walk would help. And you might as well come up here and go play with Sid and Shane, I know you're there."

Lex came out of the tree line with a sigh. "Well, next time don't try to duck out when I'm putting Gabby down." He stopped to send Megan a narrow-eyed look. "You all right? Shane said your blood pressure was up. I heard you weeded!"

"She sat while Gabby and I weeded. She held Mr. Man here and he never cried once. *Hmpf.* You think I'd make your sister weed when she's been sick?"

Lex's manner softened as he brushed a hand down Nina's jawline. "All these years and it still gets me hot when you snap at me."

Nina actually blushed. "Go on then. We got girl talking to do."

"Fate is pretty awesome." Megan looked around at them, her sisters, her friends, at her deck in her yard. Awesome indeed. Hard fought, but worth every moment of struggle.

* * * * *

Acknowledgments

Thank you so much to the entire Carina Press team! Art, editorial and marketing/promotion—you're all fantastic. I appreciate how much you do for me and my books.

Angela James—Thank you for everything.

About the Author

The story goes like this: While on pregnancy bed rest, Lauren Dane had plenty of downtime, so her husband took her comments about "giving that writing thing a serious go" to heart and brought home a secondhand laptop. She wrote her first book on it before it gave up the ghost. Even better, she sold that book and never looked back.

Today Lauren is an award-winning *New York Times* and *USA TODAY* bestselling author of over sixty novels and novellas across several genres.

Find out more about Lauren's books at www.laurendane.com.

Twitter.com/LaurenDane
Facebook.com/AuthorLaurenDane

This is for all you wonderful readers who have supported and loved my Cascadia Wolves so much.

Author's Note

Reluctant Mate was originally published some years ago with the title *Reluctant*. It's a prequel novella to *Pack Enforcer*, so if you're starting here, the world will bloom in the next book—which opens ten years later.

While I've cleaned it up, the story remains the same.

The world of the Cascadia Wolves is connected to my other paranormal romance series. For reading order and information about how they're all related to one another, head on over to my website: www.laurendane.com/faq.

RELUCTANT MATE

Chapter One

Seattle, Washington, 1996

Layla Warden pulled her brand-new BMW into her spot in the parking garage. She'd just gotten the parking spot and the big raise that paid for the flashy new car at the financial firm that'd hired her straight out of college three years before.

Getting out, she headed to the bank of elevators and smoothed down the skirt of the suit she'd picked up from Brooks Brothers the weekend prior. Her hair was perfectly cut every six weeks, without fail, and her manicure was flawless. Layla Warden had a ten-year plan and things were going quite well.

No one she worked with had the slightest idea that she turned furry and ran through the woods hunting rabbits every few weekends, and she planned to keep it that way. Humans tended to get a bit shirty when confronted with the existence of werewolves. Most werewolves she knew weren't very out about it. It kept them all safer.

Her human life was kept separate from her life as a member of the ruling Pack family. Most of her social life was with her Pack and family while her work life was absent that altogether. Her family was not incredibly pleased with the distance she kept her professional life from the Pack. They wanted her to hook up with a male from the Pack and settle down. They felt she could do that better if she worked for one of the Pack businesses. And she could understand their wishes. Who knew what her other sisters would end up doing? Tracy was a wild child at just fourteen and the twins, Megan and Tegan, had decided at eighteen to become part of their older brother Lex's Enforcer guards. Clearly their parents looked to her to continue their line. But they'd have to wait.

The last thing Layla wanted right then was a mate. Ugh. She didn't want that intense connection to anyone just yet. Werewolves didn't just marry each other, they mated. They had an intense chemical and metaphysical bond to their spouse. At some point in the future that would be what she wanted, but right then Layla had plans! Those plans didn't include bossy werewolf males meddling in her day-to-day life. She had two domineering, control-freak brothers and enough other male relatives to know life mated to a werewolf male wouldn't be easy.

She loved her freedom and she liked dating around. Because she may be button-down on the outside, but Layla did love sex, and the thought of getting it from just one guy forever? That didn't appeal at all.

Still, she appreciated her roots and her upbringing. She wasn't ashamed of being a werewolf, but she also didn't make it her entire life like her oldest brother Cade, the Pack Alpha, did.

"Good morning, Ms. Warden."

Layla smiled at her secretary and took her mail into

her office. Her new, bigger corner office. That hadn't even been due to happen until year five of the ten-year plan and here she was at year three. Booting up her computer with a satisfied sigh, she began her work day.

And by the end of it, some ten hours later, she left the office feeling way too tired to go out like she'd promised her best friend.

When Layla got to the front doors of her building, Tia was waiting there, already dressed up, looking amazing as always and sporting an expression that told Layla any excuse she'd been planning on making to get out of the evening wasn't going to be entertained.

The petite blonde narrowed her eyes at Layla and put a hand on her hip. "I knew you'd try to get out of tonight. I can see it in your face right now. But we both need the distraction so I'm here to bug you mercilessly until you give in."

Sighing, Layla rolled her eyes and waved her through the doors after she'd unlocked them. "How much can I pay you to go away?"

"Shaddup. You're coming out with me tonight. You work twelve hours a day! You need to play a little. You're too uptight as it is. So let's see what you have in your closet. I'll pick out an outfit for you while you shower." Tia shoved her toward her bathroom and then headed off to root through the closet to find what Layla was sure would be the most revealing outfit she owned.

Even as she thought it she laughed. Tia Mathers had been her best friend since third grade. They'd gone to college and roomed together and basically shared just about everything. It helped that Tia and her family were part of Cascadia Pack too.

The best thing about Tia was that she knew a side of

Layla most people didn't. People thought of Tia as the fun-loving one while Layla was the serious one—they didn't know that Layla had a fun side too. It just got a little lost sometimes, especially since she'd gotten promoted at work.

Going into her bedroom after the shower, Layla saw that on her bed lay a pair of leather pants and a tank top.

"Are you kidding me? That's a Halloween costume!" Layla had gone to a party as Catwoman two years before and probably hadn't worn the pants since. "I'm sure I *will not* be able to get my ass into them now."

"Oh stop crying and try them on. They looked good on you then and hell, woman, I'd be surprised if you even ate today. You're getting skinny since you work all the damned time."

Giving in, Layla tried the pants on and Tia was right. They fit quite well and Layla had to admit she looked pretty sexy in them.

"Okay, okay. But no tank top. I can't wear a bra with one. You know how I hate when straps show and goodness knows me without a bra is a challenge to gravity."

"Fine. Wear this one." Tia tossed her a bright red, shimmery, short-sleeved blouse that was tight across the bodice but loose around the waist.

By the time they'd left the condo, Layla's hair was tousled in a sexy style and she wore red lipstick to match the blouse and teetered on spiky heels.

"Before you complain, we're going to Nautica. I made reservations."

Nautica was a werewolf hot spot. Members only. Tia loved it, Layla tolerated it for Tia.

"I thought you said I was supposed to play tonight?

Now I'll be hounded by power-hungry males who want to fuck their way into my family."

"Oh my god! Lay! Have you *looked* at yourself? You're gorgeous. They want to fuck *you*. Some of them are hot to be married into the Warden family but most of them want to bed you because you're beautiful, sexy and have a good job."

It was an old argument and on most days Layla could believe Tia, but it was hard being from an influential family. People assumed things. They assumed she got her job through her connections instead of the fact she'd graduated at the top of her class, interned and then worked part-time at her company for three years. They assumed her money was family money. There was money there but it was all tied up in trusts. What she and her siblings had they'd all earned.

"Okay. Fine." She knew she was being selfish and she gave in. Tia didn't date too many humans. She didn't think it was fair to have to hide such a large part of herself from them. Werewolf-only clubs like Nautica were the few places she could meet wolf males her age.

"Good. Life would be so much better if you just agreed with me from the start and I didn't have to argue with you. Because you know I'm right."

Layla rolled her eyes when they pulled into valet and flashed their membership cards. "It's 1996! What is up with the mullets?" Layla whispered this quietly to Tia before they got to the top of the stairs leading into the restaurant and lounge area.

Tia looked back over her shoulder at the group of male wolves clustered near the front doors, several with the "short on the top, long in the back" hairdo that puzzled both women. "Werewolves and their mullets! I don't know, but I'm sure glad Cade got rid of his. Your brother is hot stuff but man did he look stupid."

The two of them dissolved into laughter and the hostess just smiled at them as if they were a bit soft in the head as she led them to their table.

One thing Layla did like about the place was that due to the sheer number of wolves on-site, they piped a neutralizer for pheromones through the air-circulation system. So there wasn't a whole lot of sniffing going on. She thought it was tacky when some guy she'd just met started sniffing on her.

Across the room, Sid Rosario watched the tall, very busty redhead enter the room and sit down. Her hair was tousled around her shoulders like she'd just rolled out of bed and very big china-blue eyes took in the room around them. And damn, but the woman did leather pants well enough to make him want to lick her like a giant ice-cream cone.

"Who is that?" Sid asked his cousin Adam.

Adam peered around Sid's shoulder. "The tall one with the red hair is Layla Warden. The petite one is Tia Mathers. Layla is Pack royalty. She's the oldest daughter. Tia's just smoking hot."

"I'm not interested in her pedigree. But I'd sure like to get to know her better. You know either one of them?" Sid could not take his eyes from Layla Warden's mouth with that shiny red lipstick painting it. His cock throbbed in anticipation as a picture of red lipstick marks at the base of it flashed through his mind. Lipstick kisses on his cock, yeah, that worked.

"Ah, it's like that, is it? Well, many have tried and

failed. She's a bit cool. Tia and I dated a few times. Let's go. I'll introduce you." Adam stood and Sid followed.

"Ah, so soon?" Tia murmured to Layla. "Adam Rosario. I have very fond naked memories of him. And who is that with him?"

Layla looked up from the menu and locked gazes with tall, dark and dangerous. The man just oozed rebellion. Short black hair, a row of earrings in his right ear. Nautica had a strict dress code but despite the black jeans and the button-down shirt, she was sure the guy lived in ripped jeans and Clash T-shirts.

So utterly not her type. This thought seemed to escape her as she looked into those big hazel eyes.

"Tia, gorgeous. Long time no see."

Tia smiled up at Adam and batted her lashes a bit. "Hi."

"Hey, Layla. You look great too. Can we join you?"

Tia accepted before Layla could speak. But she wouldn't have refused anyway. Mr. Rebel made her all tingly. And it had been a while. Four months to be exact.

"This is my cousin, Sid. He's visiting here for a few weeks. Sid, this is Tia Mathers and Layla Warden."

Sid shook hands with Tia, but it was fleeting compared to the full-on, deep, soul-shaking look he gave Layla. Taking her hand, he kissed the knuckles and the warmth of his lips shot straight to her pussy.

"It's very nice to meet you, Layla. I like that name. Is it…"

"Yes. My parents were big Eric Clapton fans when I was conceived. Let's speak of it no more."

Her smile was flirtatious and Sid smiled back.

"So what are you doing while you visit? Where do

you call home?" Layla felt like she couldn't look at him enough.

The server came and took their orders and Sid watched as she sipped her drink.

He cleared his throat. "I'm doing a mural—I'm an artist. I live in Tucson. And what do you do?"

"I'm in financial services. I do portfolio planning."

His eyebrows rose.

"What? Too Yuppie for you?"

He laughed. "No, not at all. I love smart women. I'm impressed."

She relaxed.

All through dinner she felt herself being pulled under his spell. Each time he reached out to grab the salt or his beer, he'd touch her in some small way. His total attention was on her at every moment. His voice was low and seductive, an aural caress. When she spoke, he listened intently, clearly interested in what she had to say.

And she couldn't deny she was fascinated by him. Watched his hands move expressively while he talked about his work. Saw the delightful light in his eyes, making it clear he loved what he did. He flattered her and made her laugh.

There was no doubt for either of them that they'd end up in bed. She liked that his surety wasn't smug or smarmy. He was a sexy guy in town for a few weeks— the perfect fling. She certainly had no plans to stop the inevitable.

Walking out to the cars, he pulled her aside. "Can I give you a ride home? Or would you like to come back to my hotel?"

The salt air of low tide tickled her senses along with

his scent. Male werewolf did indeed smell hella good to her, and nary a mullet in sight.

"Where are you staying?"

"The Alexis."

"Let me just tell Tia. I'll be right back."

He watched as she walked over to her friend and hugged her goodbye. Tia winked at her, and Layla gave her the finger, amusing him.

"Let's go."

Adam nodded discreetly and Tia offered him a ride home.

On the way to the hotel, Sid asked if she minded him smoking a clove cigarette.

She shrugged. "I like the smell in small doses."

And it seemed to add to his spice, the very alluring masculine scent of him. God, she had it bad. She wanted to rip his clothes off and climb on his cock right there on First Avenue.

He must have noticed her near-panting and the glaze of desire in her eyes because he took her hand and kissed the fingertips. "I know. I want you too."

She shivered at the near growl in his voice, and when they arrived he tossed the keys at the valet and they headed inside quickly.

"I can't touch you yet," he said in the elevator. "Once I do, it's over."

They walked side by side, just barely not touching as they hurried down the hallway to the door of his room. Which he opened up in record time.

Taking a deep breath, Layla walked in and he followed her, careful to put the Do Not Disturb sign on the door before he shut and locked it.

Chapter Two

A long look settled between them until suddenly he was there, hands on her body, lips on hers. Everywhere he touched, her skin warmed and tingled.

His lips, lush and soft, devoured her in kiss after devastating kiss. Lust and desire drowned her, pulled her under, and she went willingly, giving in to the exquisite sensations.

When his tongue stroked in between her lips like a lover, a deep shudder broke through her. Her nipples hardened to the point of pain and her clit throbbed. His taste, warm and spicy, slithered through her, marking her senses. Her entire body began to vibrate with need. She'd never felt anything like it before. It was overwhelming but amazing too.

Needing to ground herself in him, her hands slid up the wall of his chest and began to unbutton his shirt. He hissed when she brushed against bare skin as she shoved it down his arms. Like most werewolves, he ran very warm and she felt the heat of his skin when his shirt was stripped off. His muscles bunched and relaxed under her palms. Her hands skimmed up his neck and she allowed herself a moment to glory in the feel of the silk of his hair sifting between her fingers.

Stepping back, she drank him in as she reached down and pulled her blouse up and over her head.

He was tall and lanky. Not skinny really. Lots of upper-body power there. Lean muscle roped tightly over his chest and arms. His stomach was flat and she grinned when she saw it was tattooed.

"What? Am I your first bad boy?"

"Is that what you are, Sid? I can't wait to see just how bad." She laughed then and delighted in his gasp as she shrugged out of her bra and ran her hands up her stomach and over her breasts.

"Would it please you to be my first bad boy?"

"Honey, *you* please me. I couldn't care less if you had a line of fifty bad boys at the door because you're here with me right now. And good god your tits are amazing."

Smiling again, Layla ran fingertips around her nipples in slow circles, catching her lip between her teeth for a moment. "My sister would love that tattoo."

"That so? Well, I think I'm with the right Warden sister just now." Taking two steps back to her again, he reached out and pulled her hands away, replacing them with his own.

Her breath caught at his intimate touch as he slowly brushed his palms over the sensitive flesh of her nipples.

"Well, that's good. She's fourteen anyway. But all she talks about are tattoos. And that topic is over now." Her head dropped back as his lips slid over the column of her neck and across her collarbone.

The sound of her zipper sliding down rang through the room and up her spine. He moved away from her neck and stepped back.

"Okay, I'll get my pants off, you get yours off. Meet you back here in a few seconds."

Laughing, Layla shoved her pants—not an easy feat with leather—and her panties down, pulling them off once she'd kicked out of her shoes. By the time she was naked and looked back to him, he'd just tossed his jeans and briefs to the side.

"Well." Her breath rushed out of her as she took him in. Long, lean and powerful muscle covered his body from head to toe. His cock stood so hard it tapped his flat belly. She wasn't sure but she thought she might have made a cartoonish gulp.

Which seemed sort of odd to her. He was so *not* her normal type. She liked her men in suits and ties. This man was all artsy and tattooed. Still, she was quite sure she'd never needed to have sex with anyone more than this man right then.

"If you aren't touching me very soon I might die," she whispered and then he was back against her.

"Oh god!" His words were nearly a moan as their naked bodies touched, skin to skin. If he hadn't taken a fistful of that lush red hair, he was sure his hands would have shaken with desire. Need roared through every single cell in his body. He had to have this woman and he had to have her right then. Tipping her head back, he dipped down for another kiss, this one far less controlled than the last. This one was barely leashed desire as mouths strained against each other, tongues sliding, his imitating the in-and-out motions of sex. Teeth caught bottom lips and breath mingled along with soft sounds of pleasure.

Her mouth felt so good against his, her body fit so right clutched against his that he thought it would be delightful to spend several hours doing nothing more than kissing her over and over. He wanted to spend an entire Sunday afternoon making out with Layla Warden.

But right then, his body demanded a hell of a lot more than long, slow, wet, drugging kisses. "I have to have more," he murmured and walked her backward to the bed, tipping her back onto it. He stopped, stunned at her beauty as he loomed above her. Big blue eyes blinked up at him, her hair spread around her head like a fiery halo, lips swollen from kisses.

He scented her desire and it wrapped around him with great force, nearly bringing him to his knees. He'd never reacted this way to a female, always prided himself in his slow, devastating seduction of his partners. But this one, god, he wanted to eat her up in three big bites.

On hands and knees, he arranged her on the bed so he could kiss down her neck and finally taste her nipples.

Layla looked up at him as he stared down into her face. The need etched into his features took her breath away. Her pussy bloomed, softened and slicked at his perusal. She could smell it, the spice of her arousal, and satisfaction took hold when she watched his nostrils flare and his pupils widen. *She* made him feel that way.

When his hot, wet mouth reached her nipples she thought she'd come right then. Each pull brought the sensitive flesh against the edge of his teeth and he came behind with his tongue, swirling over her nipple to soothe the sting.

She tried to reach his cock but he pulled off her nipple and looked into her face. "No. If you touch me I'll come. And I want to be in your pussy when that happens."

Before she could respond he was kissing his way down her stomach and through the sensitive crease where leg met body. Strong, work-calloused hands spread her thighs, opening her up as he stared.

"But first, I need you to be ready. Nice and wet for my cock."

"Oh!" Incoherence washed through her as he slid his thumbs through the furls of her sex, spreading her honey. "I… I'm wet now. You should fuck me. Oh god." If his thumbs, pressing up and over her clit, felt this good, what would his mouth feel like? She hoped to find out very, very soon.

His chuckle spread over her, warm and sticky. Her nipples hardened and her hips churned, needing him to touch her.

"You'll be even wetter when I'm finished." Leaning his head down, he took a long lick, dipping his tongue deep into her body and then up and around her clit. One of his thumbs slipped into her while the other slid down to stroke over her perineum and ever so lightly against her rear passage.

The tip of his tongue circled 'round and 'round her clit, getting closer to it each pass until he finally began to flick it with gentle, insistent strokes. That wet slide of flesh against her clit shocked into her body, making her back arch.

Layla's fingers dug into the bedspread as her thigh muscles began to burn from the trembling. Endorphins began to flow, her clit throbbed, orgasm was so very close. He ate her pussy like a starving man relishes a meal. She wasn't new to the act but it had never been this good before. Never felt so completely all-encompassing. Never had it rendered her helpless against the sensation.

Low, feral-sounding growls trickled from her mouth, coming from deep in her gut. Her hips began to roll, grinding herself into his mouth. She needed to come. Needed this man to make her come.

And when he grazed his teeth over her clit ever so lightly and sucked it into his mouth, flicking the underside over and over and over, orgasm hit with near violent force. Her back bowed with electric intensity as pleasure swamped her, dizzied her, intoxicated her and made her limbs heavy.

Each time she thought it was over, another wave hit. His mouth wasn't even on her anymore and still the ripples of climax sounded through her.

Dimly, she felt him pick her body up and she blinked herself back to a basic level of attention when he plunged her body down on his cock in one movement. This set off another round of aftershock orgasms, little but deep. A pleasured cry ripped from her gut as ecstasy gripped her again.

When she came back to herself she was wrapped around him, her back against the wall as he fucked her while standing.

Each roll of his hips made his abdominal muscles ripple against her pussy and shudders worked through her.

"Fuck. Fuck. Fuck. You feel so good. I don't know how long I'll last this way." His voice was tight with tension and desire. His cock sliced through her over and over, invading her body even as it welcomed him. She was so hot and wet, every muscle and synapse firing and absorbing the exquisite pleasure he delivered.

His scent tickled her senses and drove her to writhe
against him.

"Hey, fuck! I'm really not going to last when you
do that."

"Potty mouth! And we have all night. Come now.
Take the edge off and you can have me again. And
again. And again after that." Her lips brushed against
the sensitive flesh of his ear as she said it. "You know
you want to come inside me. Mark me."

Wolves didn't carry STDs and she was on birth control. She loved the feel of his naked cock buried inside
her and she knew without a doubt that she stirred primal werewolf instinct when she told him to come in her
and mark her. She was playing with fire and the danger
turned her on. She'd examine this completely out-of-
character behavior when she got home in the morning
but for right then, she'd ride it and him and enjoy it all.

"Oh you're going to pay for that, little girl. I'll enjoy
every minute of it too." His voice had deepened and
roughened as his wolf came closer to the surface. Layla's own wolf sensed it and stirred within her. Every
nerve in her body lit up as their primal selves rose and
stroked over the other's while their human skins did the
same. Never in her life had sex been so intense and all-
encompassing. She wanted more.

Leaning in, she took a deep breath where his neck
met shoulder and bit down, hard. A deep growling moan
came from him and his cock began to pulse deep inside
her as he continued to thrust through his climax. His
scent hit her straight in her gut. She wanted more of it.
Needed more of it.

And it hit her as her wolf wanted to roll around with
him all over the floor. It occurred to her just why she'd

been so intensely attracted to him, and their eyes met as the bond began to form. Glimmering threads of connection drew their DNA and their hearts and souls together. She'd just been claimed. By her mate.

Sid Rosario, a man she'd met just hours before and had just wanted a brief, fun fling with, was her fucking mate. How could she not have known? The neutralizer in Nautica, the clove cigarette and her damned lust for this guy had totally blinded her.

"Holy shit," he said wondrously as his knees buckled and he stumbled back to the bed, collapsing on it, still embedded inside her.

"Holy shit?" She tried to move away but he wouldn't let go of her and her legs weren't working well anyway. "Is that all you've got to say? You've just claimed me!"

"Why are you so pissed off? You wanted me to fuck you, Layla. And thank god, because we've found each other."

"I don't want to be found." She heaved a sigh as she felt his feelings as acutely as her own. "I just wanted to have a fun few weeks with a hot guy from out of town. I have plans, Sid."

He frowned and annoyance burst through her as she found that attractive too. His frown changed into a wicked grin and she groaned. Damn it, he'd feel her through the bond. Know how much, even as she was livid, she wanted him to take her again and again after that.

"Oh ho! This bond link thing is pretty cool. Well, we can play the 'fuck the hot stranger from out of town' game all you like, honey. Because you can't buck reality. You're my mate. And I'm yours and you just got served!" He chuckled. "I wasn't expecting it either but

I'm not going to lie and say I'm disappointed. You're beautiful and you smell heavenly. I look forward to getting to know my wife better."

Her legs had finally begun to work again and she scrambled away from him. "I'm not your wife!" She moved to grab the clothes she'd tossed all over the room, suddenly needing to be dressed.

"You're my wife. Look, Layla, I get that you're surprised. I am too. But you're a werewolf, you know the realities of our existence. You can't pretend away a mate bond. Especially not once the claiming occurs. Now that I've come inside you, we're united. You need my presence, I need yours. And we'll need the tri-bond to protect you."

The tri-bond? Oh hell no. He not only wanted to claim her entire life but she'd have to have sex with some male of his choosing too? "No, Sid. I'm not going to let this stupid metaphysical shit call a halt to my life. I like my job. I like my condo and I'm not going to move to Arizona, join another Pack and give up everything because I'm a female wolf."

"Layla, you don't have to move to Arizona. I realize your family is here. I'm a fifth son, it's not like I can't relocate. I paint, which I can do anywhere. I'm not asking you to give up your life or your job. I haven't seen your condo but we may need to get something bigger so I can have studio space. I'm a male werewolf but I'm not a caveman. I don't want to *take over* your life. I want to *share* it."

Why was he so fucking reasonable? Their whole lives as they knew them were now over.

"I need some time, okay? I need to think and I can't do it here." She got her bra and shirt back on and after a fruitless search for her underpants, she gave up, shimming back into her pants without them.

Needing to escape and think, she headed for the door, but he moved to it first. "Where are you going?"

"Home. I'm going to my condo. I need to think. Please."

"Let me drive you."

"No. I'm not that far, I'll catch a cab out front. I know the number here, I'll call you. Just give me some space."

"Space? Layla, you're my mate. The claiming has been made. This isn't something you can think away."

"Look," she struggled to speak without her voice breaking as her world crashed in around her. "I have plans! I can't think here with you...with your scent and your taste in my mouth. It's too much and I have to work this out. On my own." She looked up into his eyes. "Please."

His face softened and he pushed a tendril of her hair out of her face. "Wait," he ordered, and grabbed a piece of paper from the desk and shoved it at her. "Give me your address and your phone number. I'll give you until Sunday. You'll need the tri-bond. The longer you wait, the more dangerous it becomes. For both of us."

Sighing, she took the paper and wrote the info down. "I'm in Queen Anne. Just like two miles away."

"I'm a very patient man, but even I have limits. Neither of us was expecting more than a brief thing, I know that. But you can't fight biology and if you look into yourself, you'll find you don't want to."

Kissing her softly, he stepped away from the door to let her go. She felt how difficult it was for him and before she could stop herself she reached out and caressed his face. "Thank you."

Quickly, before she could change her mind, she left and headed home.

* * *

And ended up feeling like shit all day as she didn't answer her phone and tried to think. But she couldn't focus on anything other than Sid. The way he felt against her, the way his mouth felt on her, the way his cock filled her. More than the sex, she wanted to smell him, to be with him, to know him. And even though she'd showered off the scent of their sex, the claiming and their bond changed her essential scent subtly and each time she breathed in she was reminded of him.

Damn it! She didn't want to be subsumed into someone else's life. Okay, so she didn't want to want it. But now that she'd been with Sid, she wanted him in her life.

After a day of pacing and reaching to call the Alexis about a thousand times, she drove to Ballard and showed up on Tia's doorstep.

"Whoa! What happened to you last night?" Tia grinned and let Layla into her house. "You're not the one-night-stand type and oh fuck…" Tia's grin fell away and her eyes widened as she scented the bond.

"Yes. Oh god, Tia. What am I going to do?" Layla tossed herself onto the couch.

"What do you mean? Did he treat you badly? That fucker, I'm going to track him down and rip out his throat!"

Layla stopped her whining and looked to Tia with a laugh that came unbidden at the way she was always so steadfastly on her best friend's side. "No! He's…he's great. Sweet, really good in bed, funny. He's fine with the bond. He's happy about it even."

"Wait, you're bitching because of what, then?"

"Tia, I have *plans*! They don't include being mated to a painter! I need to mate with a stockbroker. We'll have two children and live in Maple Leaf or Ravenna. In like, five years." Even as she said it she knew she didn't mean it, never had, really.

Tia snorted and rolled her eyes. "Those plans are not you. You *think* they're you because that's your way of being different from the other Wardens. I've known you since we were nine years old. You're only button-down on the outside. Not that stockbrokers can't be hot, but your mate isn't one. God, some wolves wait twenty years past maturation to find a mate and you find one at twenty-five and you're complaining? He's hot! And he's good with the bond? And anyway, how did you get away? 'Cause it's hard for me to see a werewolf male just letting you walk away. And oh my, the tri-bond?"

The tri-bond was a ritual whereby a third wolf, a relation of the male mate, or a Packmate who ranked higher than he did, formed a bond with the female. It created what was termed as an anchor bond for two important reasons. To keep the female from losing herself in the emotional and hormonal surge of the claiming and also to keep her alive should something happen to her mate. The bond between mates was so strong that should something happen to the male, without the tri-bond, the female would die too. It was sort of a stabilizing connection. Like a surge protector, her brother Cade always said.

Layla let her head fall back against the couch cushions with a groan. "I know! Look, I'm not saying a threesome with two hot dudes is a bad idea in general. But I just met Sid and now I'm going to have to have sex with one of his relatives or something? Ugh! Adam? No, no, no! I can't have sex with someone you've had sex with."

"Okay, so I get the point about Adam. But you know you need the tri-bond to anchor you. You *know* that. It's not random sex, the Anchor is a necessary thing. Without him you'll slip into insanity and that's no joke. The longer you wait, the worse it'll get."

"Why now? God, Tia, I just got this promotion and my life is going so well. This just complicates everything!"

"Oh shut up!" Tia got in her face. "You are *not* this person. Stop whining. Accept reality. He's your mate. Period. And you need the tri-bond or you'll both be in trouble because once you go, he'll lose it too. And for what? This stupid, selfish tantrum?"

Layla looked up at her friend, stunned. Stung, she pushed off the couch and headed for the door. "I shouldn't have come here. I expected you to support me."

"Support you in what? Being stupid? Not dealing with the thing you need to keep you from going insane? I *am* supporting you, Lay. This guy is your mate. You said yourself that he's funny, good in bed and nice. He's fine with the bond. You're *lucky*! Instead of dealing with it like you usually do, you're throwing a tantrum. You can't change anything with this behavior. This drama queen thing is a sign."

"A sign? What are you talking about?"

"The longer you go unanchored the less rational you'll be. Look at yourself! You're a take-charge person. You rarely ever whine about things. You deal. Period. I'm worried about you, Layla. You aren't yourself right now."

"I'm fine." Taking satisfaction in the sound of the door slamming behind her, she left.

Chapter Three

Layla stomped out to her car and drove east while she reeled, trying to process everything that'd happened. She'd worked so hard to advance at her job. It was difficult being taken seriously as a woman in her field. And she was young, another thing she'd had to overcome. A curvy red-haired woman who was young and attractive wasn't something she complained about being in her day-to-day life, hell, it opened doors for her, she knew that. But it was hard to get past in the corporate world.

Three days before she'd been focused on her career and there had been nothing but clear pavement between her and another promotion. But with a mate she now had to navigate around how yet another person would react to her choices. It was hard enough dealing with her mother who never stopped complaining that she spent too much time on her career and not enough time on her family. Now she had to deal with a man. Not a man, *the* man.

And here she was with a big old wrench thrown into her plans by that man! As it was, all she could think about was Sid Rosario. She wondered if he was upset or hurt by her running off. She didn't want this. She wanted her old life where she was free to stay late at work, free to work on a Sunday, free to get up and work in the middle of the night if she needed to.

She wasn't some human who had no idea what she was in for. She was born a wolf, had seen wolves around her mate and watched their lives change in revolutionary ways. Was she ready for that? Did she even want to be? Was she ready for the level of dedication and involvement from her mate? Her DNA was now altered with his claiming of her. She was changed forever.

Frustrated and frightened, she slammed a palm against the steering wheel.

She needed to run. Running always calmed her, and she felt her wolf begin to agitate within her, needing release. Maybe she could think of a way around this mess if she could get a little bit of calm and stop obsessing about Sid for a few minutes.

Pulling her car onto a side road near where Cade's new house in the woods was, she hid her things in the wheel well and went to the tree line to shed her clothing. The scent of the wild teased her senses, soothed her as she fell to her knees and let her wolf take over her body.

Her humanity slid away as her fur rose and the world was black and white and gray and yet sharp and vivid. The scent of her surroundings painted the air—the moss on the trees, the mushrooms in the dead tree trunk, the squirrels and the rabbits that scurried out of the way as they scented her.

Nose up, she drew in the universe through her senses and the world was suddenly right again. There, covered in a pelt coppery and fiery red and gold, things were simple again.

And she ran.

* * *

Sid hung up the phone, pissed off. He'd been trying to call Layla for the last day and a half and even had showed up at her place, and there was no sign of her. Her scent, now *their* scent, was cold enough that he could tell she hadn't been around since early the day before.

He paced, his wolf agitated and worried. He never should have let her leave. A newly bonded female wolf needed the tri-bond, and each hour that passed without it happening put her in danger and made her less rational. She was already surprised and stressed out and that would only be exacerbated by the lack of the anchoring bond.

He picked up the phone and dialed Adam, who told him where Tia lived and that he'd meet his cousin there.

Not knowing what to expect, Sid was happy Tia seemed so happy and supportive of the bond. He was less happy to hear about Layla's agitation and that it seemed so far out of her normal character.

It wasn't just that he wanted to protect her—he *needed* to protect her. As a male werewolf, the mate bond was the ultimate commitment. Her needs were paramount. Knowing she was out there somewhere, upset and agitated, tore at him.

"Do you have any idea where she could be?"

"She always runs when she's upset and Cade, my Alpha and her brother, has a big house on a lot of acreage. She may have headed up there."

"Will you show me? Adam, will you go back to my hotel? I'll need an Anchor and I'd be honored if you were our tri-bond."

"No! Look, part of what had Layla upset was the

thought of having sex with someone I've…had sex with. Do you have any other cousins or family members who could help? Any other Pack members who outrank you?"

"I hadn't thought of it that way." Sid looked at Tia and thought. "Adam, call Shane please. He's on break from school visiting Aunt Jennifer down in Portland. I just talked to him a few days ago. Will you ask him for me? I need to go and get her."

Adam agreed and said he'd arrange for their cousin Shane to meet them at Sid's hotel room for the tri-bond.

They took Tia's car and drove up to where she thought Layla may be, pointing out Cade's new house.

"She won't have gone up to the house. They'd scent her and know and make her deal. I'm going to take you down this back road here to see if her car is around. You'll have to do the rest. There're about forty acres of forest here."

"I'll scent her if she's here." He meant to bring her back and make her safe, one way or another.

Tia swore when she saw Layla's car. "There's her car right there. Do you want me to wait?"

"No. Because if she gets away from me, I'm going up to that house and enlisting her family to help me."

Tia laughed. "You're gonna be just fine, Sid. She's a good person. Strong. Her family is important to her. Be gentle."

"She's my mate. Of course I'll be gentle. And yeah, I can tell she's a good person. Thank you."

He got out of the car and quickly disrobed, getting to all fours and letting his wolf surface. Nose up in the breeze, he caught her scent, spicy and rich, and tore off into the trees to track his mate down and bring her back.

* * *

Layla lay next to a small stream, breathing in the deep loam of the forest floor. The calm she'd had when she first ran was leaving her. As she'd run she'd thought. A lot. Realized that all her reasons, well, most of them anyway, for resisting the mate bond were work-related. And she realized she didn't want her life to be all about work any more than she wanted her life to be all about a man. There would be a way to find a middle ground. If anyone could, Layla knew she would do it.

Moreover, Tia was right. All of her whining and drama were not part of Layla's normal behavior pattern. Her grasp on things became more tenuous the longer she went without the tri-bond. And she missed Sid.

But despite knowing she needed to get to Sid and take care of the tri-bond, worry that he'd be angry at her and not want her anymore ate at her. The weight of the fear held her in place.

She was so lost in her thoughts she didn't even sense his approach until he pounced, teeth at her throat to hold her still.

Panic filled her and her back legs levered up to push off any male but hers, until he growled, a mixture of comfort and warning. She drew in a breath and scented him. Her mate. *Hers*. She relaxed and he let go and licked over the spot where he'd bitten her.

A soft whine brought her head around and her heart pounded at the sight of him there. So large and majestic. The most beautiful wolf she'd ever seen. Leaning in, she rubbed her face along his and growled softly. The sound was filled with desire and longing.

He took her there, quick and feral. Large body over her smaller one. His need to have her and mark her as a wolf as well as a man overwhelmed her. After, they lay side by side, her muzzle resting on his back as they let the forest calm them.

After some time she transformed, human eyes looking up at him.

Moving to her knees, she reached out and ran a hand over his ebony fur, thick and soft. Putting her arms around his neck, she hugged him tight and breathed him in. Loved the smell of him. "Such a gorgeous wolf. I'm sorry I ran."

And only moments after she'd spoken, his skin was smooth and hard as he transformed back and held her with human arms. "It's okay. Shhh, it's okay. Let me take care of you, honey."

He pulled her against him, into his lap, and kissed her mouth. He felt like he'd come home in her taste. The way her hands felt as they slid up his arms and into his hair, against his skull, burned into him.

"I want to be inside you again. But we don't have a blanket so will you come back with me? To any place with a bed? We can talk afterward. We've got to get the tri-bond dealt with, and today. You understand that?"

She nodded, her eyes clear. "I was afraid you wouldn't want me anymore. That you'd be so angry because I ran."

Kissing her again quickly, he added, "God, it's so good to hold you. I've been crazy without you. I was worried, yes. I'd have brought you back kicking and screaming if I had to. But there's no way on earth I wouldn't want you. You got scared and things got a bit over your head. It's okay. I'm here and we're going to get through this together. From now on, we'll take turns freaking out so one of us will always be the strong one. You ready?"

And it was the most perfect thing he could have said. Sharing their burdens instead of shouldering them all himself—that last knot of concern in her gut eased from her softly.

"Yes. Oh yes." She allowed him to help her up and they changed again to run back to where her car was parked.

A short trip to his hotel and they practically ran to his door.

Turning on the hot water in the shower, she let his lips capture hers once again as she discarded her clothes and tossed them aside. A sense of deep rightness followed when his ended up with hers in the same pile. So odd that something so simple would make her feel her connection to him so deeply but it did.

"Come shower with me, I'm all dirty."

His lips slid into a naughty grin. "I like you dirty. It's my favorite."

Laughing, she pulled him into the stall with her, moving so he could share the hot water with her. His hands slapped hers out of the way as he took over the job of soaping her up from head to toe.

"My. I think I'll be the cleanest wolf ever when you're finished."

"As long as your insides stay dirty, I'm fine with that."

"Yeah?" A soap-slicked hand wrapped around his cock and began to slowly ride up and down the shaft.

His eyes dropped closed as he lazily accepted her touch. She added a second hand. Each hand slid up from the root of him, over the crown and head, and as the other followed to make the same path the seeds of his orgasm were sown and sensation began to build. Her scent rose on the steam, tightening his body.

Her sole focus was on him and pride burst through his senses. This beautiful, vibrant woman gave herself to him, made his pleasure her goal, and he'd never felt more amazing.

"Honey, let's get into the bedroom." His need to be inside her ramped up and his control hung by a thread. Knowing he'd have to share her, even for something as natural and necessary as the tri-bond, drove his need to have her, mark her, before his cousin arrived.

She stepped out and toweled off as he picked her up. Wrapping her legs around his waist, she teased them both, sliding her pussy over his cock.

"Still naughty on the inside, I see." Sid tossed her on the bed and she laughed as she bounced.

"With you, I seem to have a limitless supply."

"Oh good. I'm glad to know I bring the goods into this relationship."

She held her hand out to him. "Come on then. Do me before I start going crazy."

Shaking his head, he fell to the mattress next to her. "Don't joke! Damn it, Layla, I was so worried about you. Tia told me where you were. She's worried too. My cousin will be here. No, not Adam. Shane. Shane is a good guy, probably my closest male relative other than my oldest brother. He spent many summers with us when I was growing up. My brothers are all much older than I am, Shane was one of my only other cousins who was near to my age. I trust him with my life, god knows he and I got into enough trouble as teenagers. His mom is human, his dad is a werewolf. He didn't really grow up in a Pack so my parents were sort of in charge of his education as a werewolf. It's a very long story but she—his mom—lives in Portland and he's been visiting her on break from school. He goes to medical school at UCLA. Anyway, he's on his way up from Portland. We've got some alone time for now."

Pushing him back against the bed, Layla rolled atop him and rained kisses on his neck and over his chest. "Okay. I'm not happy about this. I know, I know it's necessary and all. I can feel myself losing my grip already. I'm more irrational than I normally am. But you know, I'd rather have a fun threesome, not some rigid, forced thing."

"Layla, after this, there'll be no more threesomes." His voice was a growl and the ferocity of it sent shivers down her spine. "You're mine. I don't relish the idea of you being with anyone else either. But it's our reality and what we need to do to keep you safe if something should happen to me. And so let's just make the best of it. I'll stay here if you don't mind. I can't bear the thought of it happening and not knowing."

Shimmying down his torso, she let her hair trail over his skin as she kissed and licked over his stomach. She surrounded his cock with her breasts and he groaned.

His hands slid through her hair and cradled her skull. "You're suddenly so important to me. Three days ago I didn't even know you and now you're everything."

"Hmm. A girl could get used to hearing stuff like that." Moving down farther, she licked the head of him, tasting the salty spice of his pre-cum.

"Oh yeah, well, a guy could get used to that too."

Moving to kneel between his thighs, she bent on all fours and took him into her mouth. She loved the taste of him, the feel of his skin as she licked over him.

The hot slick of her mouth on his cock began to pool sensation at the base of his spine. He'd never felt anything like it, the slide of her tongue against him. Watching down his body, he was mesmerized by the dreamy sway of her ass, each knob of her spine down the curve of her creamy back. She was exquisite, the sexiest thing he'd ever seen and felt.

He let her continue to suck his cock, watching her mouth, feeling his balls tighten against his body, knowing his climax was approaching. Each draw of her mouth and swirl of her tongue was another step higher.

Waiting until he teetered just on the edge of coming, he gently pulled her back. "Wait, honey. I want that sweet pussy around me when I come. Ride me, Layla."

Scrambling up his body quickly, she knelt over him and reached back to guide him true. That moment, suspended just above him, her hand around the girth of his cock, the expectancy of it, was sweet. She felt the heat of her pussy just above her hand and the hardness of his cock would soon fill her.

She let the anticipation build, feeling herself grow even wetter, her clit throbbing in time with her heart. Catching her bottom lip in her teeth, she looked down into his face, watching his pupils widen and the steady beat of his pulse at his neck.

"You're going to kill me."

"Wouldn't want that. I need you alive for your cock." Her voice was teasing as she slowly sank down onto him.

Sensation shot up her spine. Pleasure filled her, electric and hot, his cock the source. She arched her back to take him deeper, feeling the head nudge against her cervix as she lowered herself down on him over and over.

The muscles in his abdomen bunched and released against her inner thighs. His hands stroked over the skin of her thighs and up the curve of her waist. Her wolf pressed against her human skin and brushed against him. In answer, his wolf did the same and her skin felt tight, nearly too small as the feeling filled and filled and filled her until she thought she'd explode.

Panic began to edge against the pleasure but his soft touch and murmured words calmed her. "Shhh, honey. It's just us. Let it be." Big hands held her hips and she let go, let his calm wash over her. "That's the way, honey. I love the way you feel around me."

Her palms moved over his chest as she pulled his cock back into her pussy, deep and hard. Over and over.

Hands held her breasts, thumbs lazily moving back and forth over her nipples. Her breath hitched as she caught his gaze, looking at her with deep hunger. More deep than sexual hunger. He devoured every detail of her face, the line of her neck. His hands on her breasts were reverent.

Her honey, hot and sticky, brushed against his groin, scalded his cock. The superheated walls of her pussy gripped him, pulled him back into her body even as she rose up on her thighs and withdrew.

The sight of her, like a goddess above him, burned into his soul. One hand slid down and he drew his fingertips through the wet and swollen folds of her pussy, bringing her honey up and around her clit in big circles.

She gasped and he groaned when her pussy fluttered around him as her body readied itself for orgasm.

"You're pretty good with all your appendages there, Sid. I think I'll keep you around just to see what you can do with your elbows and nose."

A surprised laugh came from him. "So essentially, that whole suit thing is like your Clark Kent disguise?"

He sped up the fingers on her clit, moving them from side to side so it took her long moments to find words. "You have to know it's a bit hard to concentrate on your questions when you do that." She tightened herself around him and raised a satisfied eyebrow when he gasped. "Clark Kent? 'Cause I'm so super in the sack?"

"Among other things." Things shifted between them and it became a competition to see who could make the other come first. "But what I mean is that underneath the tailored clothing there's this whole other layer to you. I gotta tell you, it's pretty intoxicating."

She paused, incredibly touched, and then burst into tears.

"Honey? That was a compliment." He sounded confused and slightly worried but she noticed he didn't stop his fingertips over her clit.

"I know. I'm not usually like this. I…what you said, it just touched me. It was a lovely thing to say."

Shane couldn't get there fast enough for Sid. He knew the tears and uneven emotions were due to it being so long without the tri-bond. Still, he watched her pull herself together and relief poured through them both.

Increasing the pressure over her clit, he matched the intensity of pulling and rolling fingers at her nipple. Moaning, her head dropped forward and she began to grind herself against his fingers as she sped up her pace on his cock.

"Oh it's like that, is it?"

"Show me what you got," she panted.

And he did, gently squeezing her clit over and over between thumb and forefinger. "Come on, hot stuff, show me what your cunt feels like when it comes around my cock."

She moved so that she was directly above him, levering back on his cock instead of sitting astride him. Over and over she slammed her body back against him. He wasn't going to last much longer, but neither was she.

He reared up and bit her then, where neck meets shoulder, and pushed her into climax. Which tipped him over right with her. Blinding waves of pleasure shot through him and through their link he felt her climax as well. Ricocheting back and forth between them, their united orgasm went on and on until he was sure he couldn't take another second of it.

Finally she fell to the side, his cock still inside her body.

"I win," she mumbled.

"Hey! I won. You came first." He brushed the hair out of her face.

"Exactly. I won."

They lay there, hands all over the other, legs tangled, for some time. No talking, just taking simple pleasure in the other's presence.

The phone in the room rang and Sid leaned over her body to answer it. The conversation was short and Layla got out of bed to clean up a bit. When she came back he'd hung up.

"That was Shane. He'll be here in a few minutes."

She sat with a sigh. He smiled when he noted she was wearing his robe. "Okay."

"I know you're upset about all of this. I wish it could be slow. So you could get used to the idea of being with me."

"It's not so much being with you. I *like* being with

you. Look—" she stood up, needing to move while she worked through it all "—it's about the suddenness and then this whole tri-bond thing."

"You think it's easy for me? I have a life too, Layla!"

Her first response died as she clenched her teeth. She wanted to yell at him but it wasn't fair. "I know you do, Sid."

His anger drained from him as he saw her rein her impatience back. Getting up and going to her, he pulled her tight against his body. Her arms encircled his waist and she put her head on his chest.

"We'll make it work. I actually really do love it up here. And I've got family in the Northwest obviously."

"After we complete the tri-bond, you need to check out of this hotel and move into my condo. We'll start looking for something with studio space for you soon. We need to move forward to the next stage of our life together."

Relief. Relief that they would make it work flooded him. Now that she accepted it, he could revel in finding his mate. The thing that werewolves wait so long for had happened. And his mate was beautiful and strong and smart. It would be all right.

"Good. I hate sleeping in hotels. The last two nights, knowing you were out there but I couldn't find you, drove me crazy."

A knock sounded on the door and Layla stiffened.

"Hold on, honey. Shane's a good person. I wouldn't trust your tri-bond to just anyone." Sid went to the door and let his cousin in.

It wasn't like Layla could complain. Shane was tall and broad and shared the same black hair that Sid and Adam had.

Without preamble he approached her and hugged her, kissing each cheek. "Welcome to our family, Layla. I'm honored to serve as your Anchor."

Layla blushed like crazy. "Thank you."

Sid watched her, saw how uncomfortable she was. "I have an idea. I can tell you're really nervous about this whole thing. I don't want it to be some stilted, horrible experience. I don't want you to feel embarrassed about liking what Shane is doing. You should enjoy it."

She narrowed her eyes at him. "Okay. So what's your idea?"

He turned and rustled around in his suitcase and came back with a long silk handkerchief. "My mother. She has a thing about handkerchiefs. This one is long enough. She refers to them as 'werewolf size.'"

"Long enough for what?" Her voice went up an octave as he approached. Shane just watched his cousin with interested eyes.

Sid chuckled. "To blindfold you. That way you can enjoy yourself without guilt. You won't have to worry about who is touching you where and how to respond. You just have to feel and enjoy." And he wouldn't have to watch her eyes meet another man's as he made her come either. He held the red handkerchief up. "What do you say?"

"That's a great idea, Sid!" Shane grinned. "Layla, would this work for you? I know it's not easy. I'm a stranger and heck, Sid's not much more than one. But I'm standing here making my promise to you to be your Anchor and to step in when and if you need me. In some ways, you'll be my mate too. I want this to be okay for you."

Layla looked at them both, strong male wolves bend-

ing over backward to make her feel better about having sex with two of them. She laughed. "Twist my arm.
Okay, I'll have sex with two hot werewolves while I'm
blindfolded. But I have to give Tia the details. She'll
kill me if I don't."

Sid started for a moment and then rolled his eyes.
"Okay. You ready?" Layla nodded and he moved to her
and kissed her softly. "I don't know if you're ready to
hear this yet or not, but I love you."

She gulped air and nodded. "Ready or not, it's still
true. I love you too."

He tied the kerchief around her head, not too tight
but snug enough it wouldn't slip off and no light got in.

Layla's skin suddenly felt a hundred times more sensitive. She could smell both men and hear the rustle of
clothes being removed. And then the brush of fingertips as her robe was slipped from her body.

A hand at her shoulder and lower back guided her
back in the direction of the bed. Suddenly, lips brushed
over the back of her neck as hands slid up her stomach.
Most likely, she would have felt odd about reacting de-
pending on who was doing what if she'd seen who was
touching her. But with the blindfold, she was free to
just accept the touches and relax.

A soft sigh slid from her lips and Sid murmured,
"Let's get you on the bed, honey."

Two sets of hands helped her onto the bed and onto
her back. It was a bit disorienting to feel things and
not see them coming. With the sense of sight gone, all
she had to do was feel. Feel the warm swirl of a tongue
through her navel and down through the crease where
her thigh met her body. She'd wanted to reach out and
touch a few times but when she'd tried to move her

hand, Sid had taken her wrists and put them above her head, saying, "If you touch us, you'll know who's doing what. Let it be a mystery."

So she'd left her hands above her head and lay there as mouths and hands began to caress and touch her everywhere. Her foot was lifted and strong hands kneaded, thumbs sliding over her instep. Then a mouth laid openmouthed kisses over her ankle and the very erotic spot between her ankle and the back of her heel.

Shudders wracked her body then at the intensity of feeling. Strong hands moved up her calves, massaging and caressing. She'd fallen under the hypnotic feel of that when lips closed over her left nipple.

With a gasp, she arched and both men chuckled. If she'd really paid attention she'd have been able to figure out whose mouth was on her nipple by the laugh, but she left it all alone, falling back into the maelstrom of building pleasure.

Lips drew on her nipple in a wet suck and then nibbled, over and over again. Her breath began to come short and her hips churned absently. Until the caressing hands on her thighs found her pussy and fingertips trailed their way through the wet furls of her cunt.

Then a mouth on her for long moments, eating her like there was no tomorrow. Broad, wet licks, hungry dips into her gate with a tongue. Fucking her with it. With her eyes covered, the intensity of feeling was much greater and she was quickly on her way to another climax.

But two sets of hands turned her over and she found herself on hands and knees, ass high in the air. Excitement roared through her at being handled like that. She'd never been blindfolded before and she made it a point to remember to ask Sid to try it again with her sometime, when they were alone.

Someone moved so that he lay beneath her, his cock at the level of her mouth. Her legs were spread to either side of his legs and the other man settled in behind her, mouth on her pussy that way, fingers holding her open to his hungry licks and nibbles.

A cock tapped her lips and she took it into her mouth. She realized it was Sid beneath her at that moment but it didn't freak her out. She felt safe and secure as well as desired like a goddess with these two men.

A thumb, wet with her honey, pressed into her ass. She gasped at the invasion of it and the taboo of that part of her being breached. Moments later, teeth grazed over her clit and climax consumed her. A deep, guttural cry came from her lips, around Sid's cock.

Sid groaned beneath her and began to roll his hips, thrusting into her mouth.

And suddenly a cock, much wider than Sid's, pressed into her pussy. Hands held her hips in place as he continued to push into her until she felt his groin and the soft slap of his balls against her mound.

He waited there for a moment while Sid continued to stroke into her mouth gently but surely. When the thrusting into her cunt started again, it quickly found rhythm with Sid.

In and out of her mouth, in and out of her pussy. Her body held in place as these two men sought their pleasure. As both had given it to her. The tri-bond wasn't a scary thing at all anymore but something deeply special and important. Shane was pledging himself to her with his body and with his bond. Sid loved her enough to open their relationship up and allow this third person to create the stability she needed. It was beautiful.

Sid's hands, long-fingered and graceful, cradled her skull as he rode her mouth. With his body spread out underneath her, she felt as if it were *him* that served as an Anchor. The emotions of the bond swirled through her, dark and light, but they weren't confusing and terrifying anymore, they were enormous but wonderful and she opened herself to them, knowing she wouldn't drown because neither of these men would allow it.

And things felt *right*. After the confusion of having her carefully made plans totally fall apart, the rightness of the bond and her connection to the man beneath her body clicked into place and she knew without a doubt that they would make it work because it was meant to. Corner office at work and with this wolf at her side at home, she'd continue on a path she could feel proud of achieving. She could still be her own person within something larger than that. She could be a Warden and still be Layla. She could be Sid's wife and mate and still be Layla. She could be a successful businesswoman and still be Layla.

That revelation seemed so totally simple, even as it had eluded her for twenty-five years.

"Oh, honey," Sid murmured, pleasure tingeing his voice. He'd felt her emotions through their bond and then her satisfaction and resolution. She could feel his joy at that.

Moments later, Sid's hands in her hair tightened as he came with a long groan. Her hands cupped his balls and fingertips pressed into that sensitive spot just behind them. His taste flooded her, consumed her senses.

After he finished, she kissed his softening cock and

laid her head on his thigh, arching her back as Shane continued to stroke into her pussy.

The broad girth of him filled her in a different way than Sid did. Stretched her. Sid's hands moved to her shoulders, pushing her back into Shane's thrusts. Shane reached around and pressed two fingers into her mouth, wetting them, and moved them to her clit.

She wasn't sure she could take more but his touch was just the right amount of pressure, his thrusts into her giving the friction against his touch rather than his fingers doing it.

"Come around his cock, Layla," Sid whispered in a hoarse voice. "He'll only taste you this once, let him feel how good it is."

With a deep cry, Layla began to come again, this orgasm a deep, muscle-wrenching climax laced with emotion as well as physical pleasure.

She heard Shane's stuttered curse behind her and his thrusts got harder and deeper as he fucked into her body with ferocity.

Her nipples brushed over the wiry hair on Sid's thighs with each stroke Shane made into her. Holding on, her fingers dug into Sid's hips as Shane's cock jerked and began to pulse with his orgasm.

And when his semen began to fill her, the cacophony of the lack of the anchor bond that she'd been managing, silenced. A moment of disorientation and then it all clicked into place. She felt the fullness of her connection with Sid but also that small part that was bonded with Shane.

Gently, they helped her down to the bed and she reached up and took the blindfold off. Craning her neck, she looked up at Sid and smiled as he leaned down to kiss her. Getting to her knees, she moved to Shane and hugged him, brushing her lips over his briefly.

"Thank you both."

Sid reached over and handed her the robe, which she put on, and Shane chuckled. "Layla, it wasn't a chore by any stretch of the imagination."

Sid stood and shook his cousin's hand. "Thank you, Shane."

Shane nodded at his cousin. "I'm going to take a shower and then why don't we get all your stuff moved to Layla's. Unless you want me to go right away?"

Layla shook her head. "No. I'd like to get to know you better. Plus, I'd like for you both to meet my family. They're going to be mad enough that I did all of this without telling them, you two can protect me."

"Oh great. That's the way to start off as a son-in-law!"

"No, they'll be mad at me. But we should take Tia over there too. I need to thank her for helping you to find me and for telling me off when I needed it."

After they'd given up the hotel room to Shane and moved Sid's stuff to her condo, they picked up Tia and headed out to Cade and Lex's house for a family dinner Layla had hastily arranged.

As predicted, her family was angry she'd waited so long for the tri-bond but they all seemed to really like Sid, especially fourteen-year-old Tracy, who wouldn't stop talking about tattoos and piercings.

Epilogue

Ten Years Later

Layla watched as her children played in a now-mated, twenty-four-year-old Tracy's yard. Sid and her brothers and brothers-in-law ran around with the kids and a wildly barking three-legged dog.

"Isn't it funny how this fate thing works?" Layla murmured.

"Yeah. We all lucked out in a big way, dontcha think?" Lex's mate, Nina, watched him hungrily. Layla was sure she wore the same look whenever she watched Sid. The desire for him hadn't waned one bit in ten years.

"And to think you didn't want him at first!" Tracy laughed as Sid allowed the kids and dog to tackle him.

"I wanted him from the first time I laid eyes on him. My body knew exactly what needed to happen. My wolf knew. It was my brain that was reluctant."

"Well, two kids, ten years and a minivan later, you're the happiest werewolf soccer mom I know."

Layla threw her head back and laughed. Sid heard it and turned. Heat flared between them as their gazes locked. Thank goodness all parts of her were now on the same page. She'd want Sid Rosario until the day she ceased to draw breath.

* * * * *

Can't get enough Cascadia Wolves?
Read on for a sneak preview of PACK ENFORCER,
the next book in the series by New York Times
bestselling author Lauren Dane.

Prologue

"What the heck, Tommie? I got places to go, man," Rey said, fingers agitatedly drumming on the steering wheel.

Tommie Perkins flipped his friend the bird. "Dude, hold your horses. It's not like you got a woman or anything." He snorted in amusement at himself. "I have to check something out for Cade. Something big is going on, Reyes. It's got the hierarchy all shaken up and Lex is more nervous and paranoid than usual."

Rey snorted but kept driving. If his Alpha had business that needed tending to, he couldn't just blow it off. Even he had a sense of duty.

Tommie looked down at the scribbled address on the paper in his hand and back at the street signs. "Make a right into that parking lot. I'm going to be across the street. It shouldn't take me more than ten or fifteen minutes."

Gabriel Reyes pulled the dark sedan into the lot and parked it. He sat in the car, smoking a cigarette, and waited while Tommie ran inside to do his business. After a while he got bored listening to the radio and he made a few calls, but no one was around.

Checking his watch, he narrowed his eyes when he

saw that twenty minutes had passed and still Tommie hadn't returned. It would serve the jerk-off right if he just left him. Rey got out of the car, sucked in a deep breath of the night air and heaved an annoyed sigh when he saw Tommie talking with some men he couldn't quite see in the doorway of one of the buildings.

He resolved to make the other man buy him a beer as he watched Tommie running toward him. As he got a few feet from the car, a shot rang out and Tommie looked up at him as he clutched his side with surprised agony.

Rey saw his lips form *"run"* just before another shot rang out and hit his friend in the head. "Jesus!" he cried out, jumping back into the car. He made quick work of turning the car on, and then squealed out of the parking lot, heading to Bellevue, where his sister lived. She'd know what to do.

Chapter One

Annoyed, Lex Warden snapped his cell phone shut and let out a long breath as he took in the small cottage-style house. Once he pulled his bike onto the stand and got off, he dropped the helmet on the seat and ran his fingers through his hair to get rid of the helmet head he was sure he had after all that time riding over.

The house was light blue and someone obviously took great care of it. The lawn was neat and window boxes overflowed in a burst of red and white, standing out in colorful relief against the blue. There were raised beds along the front walk and a climbing rose snaked up a lattice off the front porch.

On the porch, a glider swing and a small table with a citronella candle. More pots of flowers and hanging baskets of greenery decorated the space. It was like a nice bit of the wild right there in the city. It gave the place a sense of calm, of refuge.

Shrugging off his amazement that anyone related to Gabriel Reyes could have such a neat and organized house, he stalked to the front door. Bypassing the doorbell, he pounded.

Moments later a tall, dark-haired woman answered and her eyes widened as she took him in.

Nina felt her mouth water as she got a load of the man standing on her porch. He was quite a specimen—well over six feet tall, blond-brown hair, deep green eyes. She swept her eyes down. His T-shirt and jeans were deceiving, they looked worn and faded but she could tell they were both designer, and the boots looked hand-made. A gold Piaget watch decorated his wrist. Jeez, his hands were huge. She had to gather herself mentally as her normally ruthlessly tied down libido roared to life. She could feel her pulse flutter and she gave herself a hard mental smack. If there was one thing in the world Nina could recognize, it was trouble. And this guy was trouble. She'd placed herself on a trouble-free diet years before and she reminded herself that he was way off the menu.

Lex raked his glance over her from head to toe. The woman, most likely the sister, had on a white blouse buttoned up to the chin and slacks with low-heeled shoes. Her hair was tightly bound up into a bun on the top of her head and she was wearing glasses. He dismissed her as a sexual being immediately. "I'm looking for Rey." His voice was blunt, manner straightforward and slightly threatening.

She gathered herself up and stood tall, back straight. "Why?"

"Why?"

"Did I mumble? You do seem to speak English. Are you having a problem with the word? Do I need to explain it to you?"

Lex barely held back a growl of annoyance. "Listen, I'm looking for Rey. It doesn't have anything to do with you. Is he here or not?"

She raised a brow but remained silent, her arms crossed over her chest.

He tried to stare her down but she just snorted and started to step back and close her door in his face. "I need to talk to him," he added quickly. He shifted his weight from foot to foot, feeling like he'd been called to the principal's office.

"Is that so? He's not here. If you want to leave him a note, I'll give it to him when I see him next." Again, she started to close the door, but he put a hand out to stop her.

"When's that gonna be?"

"Just who *are* you?" Suspicious irritation was clear on her face as she examined him again, this time with a more critical eye.

"I'm Lex Warden. A friend of his."

Understanding lit her eyes, which she narrowed at him. Lex knew for sure this wasn't a good thing.

"No you're not. I know who you are, Mr. Warden, and you are not Gabriel's friend. He's had enough people in his life leading him astray. I should know, I've cleaned up after him long enough. Get the hell off my porch and don't bother coming back." She moved her arm behind the door.

He leaned in, growling, "Listen, lady, you don't know what you're getting in the middle of."

She poked him hard in the middle of his chest. Her face was hard, gaze furious. "You did *not* just growl at me! You listen here, I don't care what the fuck you want. Don't you dare try to intimidate me with your size! Growl at me! How dare you! Get the heck out of here and do it now before I shoot you."

He'd been fascinated with her face—at the light of

ferocity in her eyes, the scent of a woman in full battle mode. He stepped forward only to feel something hard poke him in the balls. He looked down and saw the shotgun she pointed at him with her free hand. With horrified fascination, he watched as she used the hand she'd poked him with to pump the gun. He heard the unmistakable click of the ammo loading. All the while, the muzzle of the gun never left the region of his balls.

She didn't stand like a woman unused to a gun. He slid his glance back up into her face, where he met her determined and bloodthirsty gaze and felt a burst of heat bloom in his gut at the sight.

Despite his annoyance and yes, a bit of fear, he had to admit that she turned him on too. He put his hands up in surrender and took a step back. "Whoa! Let's not be hasty here. I don't want to hurt you. I don't want to hurt Rey either but I need to talk to him."

"I'm not hasty." She moved the shotgun tighter against his balls. "Test me why don't you? This is ready to roll and I've had a shitty day." She narrowed her left eye at him and her lips—very nice lips, he noticed— curled up at one side in a grin.

"Look, wolf boy, he's gone. He came by, borrowed money—" she snorted "—took money—it's not like I'll ever see it again—and headed out. Told me the Pack was looking for him, wanting to kill him. Even if I knew where he ran to, which I don't, I certainly wouldn't tell someone out to hurt him."

"I told you, I'm not gonna hurt him. I need to talk to him." *Wolf boy?* He tried his sexy smile, a smile that this frigid-looking spinster should appreciate.

"Yeah, I'm sure that works on all the puppies down at the shelter. But I don't know you from Adam and the fact that you *say* you don't want to hurt him means nothing to me."

"Come on, Ms. Reyes. Give me a break. We can help each other out here, don't you think? We can talk about it more over dinner." He cocked his head in that adorable little-boy way that his mother always melted over despite the "puppies at the shelter" comment.

She actually rolled her eyes at him and slammed the door in his face.

"Shit!" he hissed and walked back down the sidewalk to where his bike was parked. Casting a glance back at the house, he saw that the spinster was looking at him from the front windows. He tipped an imaginary hat at her as he put the key in and turned the ignition, firing the bike to life. He grunted a surprised laugh when she flipped him off in return.

Nina Reyes watched the man roar away on the Harley and closed the curtains with a sigh. Men were all the same, even if they were freaking werewolves. Okay, delicious hunks of hot, gorgeous, hard werewolf flesh that she'd love to take a ride on. Oh, did she think that out loud? She winced and reminded herself that she had a battery-operated boyfriend and that was the best kind. No fuss, no muss and it never asked to borrow money.

With a snort, she put the shotgun back on the rack and removed the pins holding her hair in place. She took off the clear-lens glasses and placed them on the table near the door and rubbed her eyes.

She knew she had the kind of looks people remembered—long curly hair, big hazel eyes, legs for miles and big boobs. So she put her hair up in a severe bun. She'd cut it once but it just accentuated her eyes so she'd given herself the pleasure of letting it stay long, even if she was the only one who ever saw it down. She wore fake glasses and buttoned her shirts to the neck and wore slacks and flat shoes. It was necessary not to call attention to herself.

She wished her brother had the same caution. Damn that Gabriel! She couldn't believe he'd gotten her into yet another mess, and this time with werewolves. It was bad enough when he'd gotten attacked in a bar fight and had contracted the lycanthropy virus. She'd stood by him, hoping that surviving the adversity would make him stronger. He'd gotten involved with the local wolf Pack and had pretty much faded from her life. She'd gotten a card here and there, he'd borrowed money a few times, but she really didn't know much about his life. And with Gabriel, no news was good news. When she didn't get calls for bail at two in the morning she took it as a sign that he was alive and well, or at least not getting caught at whatever he was doing.

But really the change had only made a morally weak man physically stronger. It wasn't altogether surprising when, out of the blue, he'd showed up on her doorstep the night before, looking like the devil himself was chasing him. He said he'd seen something he wasn't supposed to and that the Pack was going to be looking for him to kill him for it. He'd certainly seemed scared for his life. She'd begged him to call the cops but he'd only looked at her like she was crazy. In the end, she'd given him all of the cash she had on her and in her emergency kitty and he'd gone, begging her to cover for him.

Cover for him! She snorted. Cover for him with frick-fracken werewolves. She rolled her eyes. But he was her brother, all the family she had, and she couldn't very well just let him get killed, even if he was a turd.

No, she was all he had and that meant something to her still. He was hers, for better or for worse, and she'd haul his ass out of trouble again, if only so she could give it a swift kick.

Double checking to be sure she'd locked the doors—as if that could stop a werewolf—she shrugged and reached back to grab the shotgun and headed for bed.

Lex pulled his Harley into the garage and walked up the back stairs into the main house. For the first time since he'd left earlier that day, he felt relaxed. Their home was one he'd designed to serve as a refuge from Pack business. The Pack did not come to their big wooden home in the woods. There was a Pack house in town where Lex and Cade spent several nights a week but this house was theirs and theirs alone. They'd watched Pack business take over every part of their father's life and eat at their parents' marriage. Neither Cade nor Lex wanted to make that same mistake.

Lex walked down the grand hallway and heard his brother, the Alpha of the Pack, clicking on the keyboard, working as usual. He walked into the home office that looked out over the lake and flopped onto the couch. "Hey."

"Hey, yourself. Did you find him?" Cade spun in his chair to look at his brother.

Lex sighed. "No. But I met his sister."

Cade raised a brow. "Oh yeah? And? I'm guessing you charmed her into bed and she told you where he was?"

Lex barked a laugh. "Try again. She fucking pointed a shotgun at my balls and told me to get lost."

Cade looked at him wide-eyed and then burst out laughing. "No shit?"

"She looks like a librarian. Comes to the door in some prim and proper outfit, hair so tightly bound up she probably got a headache, and gives me the evil eye. Mouth puckered up like she'd been sucking lemons. The chick has Sunday school teacher written all over her.

"First she poked me in the chest! Then she told me that Rey showed up at her place—said he was being threatened by the Pack who wanted to kill him, grabbed some cash and took off. Then she told me to get out of there or she'd shoot me. I look down and she's got a shotgun planted in my crotch and the meanest look I've ever seen on a human on her face. She called me wolf boy, slammed the door in my face. Oh! And flipped me off when I was driving away," Lex said, unable to keep the admiration out of his voice.

Cade wiped a tear of mirth from his eye. "The most feared wolf in North America and a Sunday school teacher got the jump on you? Damn, I wish I could have seen it with my own eyes. You must be slipping, Lex. Clearly getting shot at and running after Rogue wolves isn't enough to keep your edge." He put his hand to his chin and pretended to think carefully. "Perhaps this woman should be our new Enforcer. Should we ask her, Lex? You can teach her kids and she can handle the firearms and take down the bad guys."

Lex shot his brother a dirty look. "Make fun while you can, dickweed. I'm telling you, despite her general level of homeliness and uptightness, she was fierce. It's kinda admirable."

"Admirable? And she's related to Rey? How come he's such a weasel then?"

"There's a messed up weasel in every family. Look at you." Lex smirked at his brother as he heaved himself off the couch and then headed down the hall to the kitchen. He bent to grab a beer from the fridge and then tossed one to Cade, who'd wandered in behind him.

"Ha ha, very funny. Call me Alpha when you say that," Cade growled. "What's your plan, then, oh scary Enforcer?" Cade asked, tossing the beer cap into the recycling and leaning back against the wall.

Shoving past Cade, Lex moved to sit down at the table. "We watch the sister. You know Rey will need help. He's going to screw up sooner or later. Hell, she admitted that she'd cleaned up after him his whole life. When he comes to her, we'll grab him." Lex took a sip of the beer and shrugged his shoulders. "We have to find out what he saw."

"Well, we'd better hope we get to him before the Rogues do," Cade said.

"For his sake and ours. We have to find out what's going on. Until we do, no one can be trusted, and you can't run a Pack that way."

Don't miss Lex and Nina's story!
PACK ENFORCER is available now wherever
Carina Press ebooks are sold.

www.CarinaPress.com

Acknowledgments

Thanks go out to Angela James and the rest of the Carina team because they do so much to make my life and my books better.

Still thanking my husband because it's still true that he's amazing (and patient).